P9-DXT-640

A MONTH
OF SEVEN DAYS

A MONTH
OF SEVEN DAYS
Shirley Climo

THOMAS Y. CROWELL   NEW YORK

Typography by Joyce Hopkins
3 4 5 6 7 8 9 10

Library of Congress Cataloging-in-Publication Data
Climo, Shirley.
    A month of seven days.

    Summary: When twelve-year-old Zoe's Georgia home is
taken over by Union soldiers, she uses all her ingenuity
to drive them away.
    1. United States—History—Civil War, 1861–1865—
Juvenile fiction. [1. United States—History—Civil War,
1861–1865—Fiction. 2. Georgia—Fiction] I. Title.
PZ7.C62247Mo 1987   [Fic]   87-5259
ISBN 0-690-04658-8
ISBN 0-690-04656-1 (lib. bdg.)

In memory of
Aldarilla S. Beistle,
who first told parts of
this story

A MONTH
OF SEVEN DAYS

Saturday
1

"I declare, Zoe!" Her mother's voice rose sharply up the stairwell. "When there's a chore to be done, you move slow as a tortoise!"

Zoe winced. A drop of ink ran down the pen and dribbled onto the paper. "Drat!" she muttered.

She had wanted this page to be perfect. If it didn't look right, maybe the charm would not work right, either. Maybe it wouldn't anyway. "I'm near done writing in my journal, Mama."

"Well, just don't you dawdle, hear?"

Zoe looked down at her book. The ink drop had spread and the date was blurred. The four had a squiggly tail dangling down like a pollywog's. She dipped the brass nib of the wooden pen into the inkpot and traced the numbers again.

Running her thumb along the seam, Zoe pressed the page flat and began the magic triangle.

Abracadabra
Abracadabr
Abracadab
Abracada
Abracad
Abraca
Abrac
Abra
Abr
Ab
A

Beneath the final *A*, as if it were the tip of Papa's own letter opener pointing to his name, she printed:

JOHN JACOB SNYDER.
MAY THIS CHARM PROTECT HIM.

Next she was supposed to fold the paper into a bitty triangle and give it to Papa to hang from a thread about his neck. He should wear it buttoned inside his shirt for safekeeping. Not a chance she could manage that, not with Papa off to war and herself stuck at home like a fly in molasses. But writing down the magic words might help him all the same, since this book was one of Papa's own ledgers. Hers, now. Zoe flipped back to the flyleaf and wrote in large black letters:

THIS JOURNAL IS THE PERSONAL PROPERTY OF
ZOE STEWART SNYDER.
NONE MAY TRESPASS IN THESE PAGES!

There. The charm would stay a secret.

"Make note of everything meaningful while I'm gone," Papa had said, and that's what she'd promised. But nothing ever happened daytimes worth the waste of ink to write it down. She'd never know if something happened nighttimes. Mama treated her like a child and hurried her off to bed as soon as it got dark.

Zoe kicked off her boots and wiggled her toes. It felt downright heavenly to free her feet. She bent down and spit on her finger, rubbing the blister on the toe that poked through the hole in her stocking.

"Shoo, FLY, don't bother me,
Shoo, fly, don't bother me . . ."

The words weren't sung. They were hollered loud enough to split her eardrum. Zoe jumped up. If it wasn't Mama plaguing her, then it was her brother. She stuck her head out the dormer window. "Jim Henry! Get down from that tree before you break your fool neck!"

The leaves on the beech stirred, and a few of yesterday's raindrops splattered down on the chickens that scratched for earthworms among the roots.

"Shoo, fly, and go scare Zo,
Tickle her bare big toe!"

3

"I know where you are!" shouted Zoe. She knew what he'd been up to, too. Snooping. Jim Henry had seen her write the charm. He'd watched her take off her boots, like as not. "Spy!"

Zoe thumped the book shut. Her brother would be right pleased if she threw it at him. He'd been itching to peek at her journal. Didn't matter he could scarcely read a word.

"If you're going to call names, kindly say mine right," she said. "It's Zo-*e*, if you please."

"Zoe-if-you-please, she's skeered of bees!
Zoe-if-you-please, she's skeered of Yankees!"

She picked up her left boot and sent it sailing into the branches of the beech tree. There was a flurry of falling twigs, and the chickens squawked in protest.

"Missed me!"

A patch of blue shinnied down the trunk and disappeared around the corner of the veranda.

"Just you wait!" threatened Zoe, but something else had caught her eye.

Her boot had landed in the honeysuckle bush, smackdab in the middle of all those hornet-bees. Even up here she could hear their hateful buzzing. She'd had two stings already this summer. And as for Yankees . . .

"Yankees are devils!" she called after him. "And if they caught hold of a sassy boy like you, they'd *eat* him!"

Let Jim Henry think about that! Zoe pulled the stick from the window, and the thick glass pane swung down

4

with a bang. Neither bees nor a pokey-nosed brother could bother her now. It was plain common sense to shut it anyway, for the sky looked fixing to rain again.

Beyond the big beech, the Georgia hills were haloes of heavy gray clouds. Bad weather for digging potatoes. Never could be any good weather for a chore like that. Zoe could already feel the sticky, slippery clay, could almost see the wriggling creepy-crawlies hiding in it. But maybe she'd be lucky. Maybe Mama would put off the digging, or ask Jim Henry to do it. As far as he was concerned, the more mud and mess the better.

"Zo-oh-eee!"

Mama's temper was frazzling. Zoe could tell by the way she said her name, like it was three whole words and not just three little letters. "Yes'm?" she answered.

"I'll not ask you again to bring in those taters. Mister Hodge needs a hand."

What Mister Hodge needed was two hands. Zoe's. "I'll be down directly."

She pulled on her right boot. Wearing but one shoe meant a year of trouble for every step you took. Still, she'd be asking for trouble right now if she kept Mama waiting. Zoe hopped down the stairs on her stockinged foot, holding on to the rail, but when she tried to walk softly down the hall, her right boot clomped on the floorboards. Might as well have announced herself with a roll of drumbeats, for Mama poked her head through the kitchen doorway.

"What in the world? . . ." She waved the big basket in her hand. "Where is your other boot?"

5

"In the honeysuckle," mumbled Zoe. "I'm just fetching it."

Mama dropped the basket with a thud. A look of exasperation replaced the puzzled frown on her face. "The honeysuckle!"

"I was—airing it out." Zoe unknotted her bonnet from its peg by the back door, keeping her back to her mother. "How come Jim Henry's not helping? I do twice as many chores as he ever does."

"You're twice as old. Thirteen before the summer's out, although I weary of waiting for you to act it." Mama sighed. "With Jim Henry so delicate, he might take a chill in this dampness."

Zoe bent over and picked up the basket. "Delicate!" she breathed.

Her mother said, "Mind you keep on your bonnet so's you don't freckle."

"Yes, ma'am." Zoe hopped out onto the stoop, banging the door behind her.

"There's no call to slam the door like that!" Her mother's voice rose. "It jars open the clock case and rattles my nerves besides. In my condition, I simply cannot credit why . . ."

Zoe did not linger to hear more. Mama's condition was plain enough. The baby-to-come bulged beneath her apron. And most of the time what Mama simply did not credit was Zoe herself.

Saturday
2

A beehive. Hornet-bees might think her boot was some new-fangled hive hung up in the honeysuckle. Dozens and dozens could be swarming in it right this minute!

"Jim Henry!" Zoe yelled. "Come fetch this boot!"

Bees buzzed in answer. There wasn't so much as a whistle from her brother. When you wanted him, he was harder to lay hold of than a shadow.

A branch, long and straight as the fireplace poker, had broken off the beech tree. Zoe picked it up and waved it like a sword. She'd never attacked bees before. With her it was always the other way around.

"Shoo!" she shouted, and stabbed at the honeysuckle.

The bush shook, and angry bees circled up from the blossoms. Zoe ducked and swung the stick again. Her boot teetered and then fell to the ground. She snatched it up and hobbled off in quick retreat.

She was safe from stings on the shady front veranda. Still, she shook the boot at arm's length before cautiously wiggling her foot into it. Nothing in the toe but the paper stuffing. She'd outgrown her own shoes months ago, but these old boots of Papa's were as big as river barges. Even if she packed them with a whole bale of cotton, they'd still rub blisters. Zoe tugged on the shoelace until the eyelets were tight together.

She picked up the basket, crossed the gravel drive, and started down the dirt lane. At the bottom of the hill, just before the lane met the road to Spring Place, two paths branched off. One trailed left through the brambles to the well house by the creek. Zoe took the path to the right, cutting down the steep slope to the lower fields. A bird scuttled through the tall weeds, alarmed by her approach. Zoe caught a glimpse of speckled feathers as the bird fluttered away. One of Mama's chickens. That hen had hidden a nest hereabouts.

"Silly old biddy!" Zoe swung the basket.

Maybe she should be looking for the nest instead of for potatoes. Shame to let eggs go to waste, with food so scarce folks had to chew each bite twice so they'd feel they'd eaten. But even from here she could make out Hodge, turning up the potatoes for her to gather. The Indian's arms went up and down, lift and dump, as his spade bit steadily into the heavy red clay. He was like the mechanical man on her brother's bank. Put a penny in the slot and the man's arm would jerk up and lift his hat. Papa had given it to Jim Henry for his sixth birthday. But it seemed an age since there'd been a penny to spare so that a little iron man might tip his hat.

Zoe went on. The wet weeds were slippery and she half slid down the hillside. Hodge looked life-sized now. Bigger, even, he was so tall. He gave her the fidgets. Hodge seemed to see right into her head and pick out her thoughts.

Mister Hodge. Papa was strict about showing proper respect. "This land belonged to Mister Hodge's people before the rest of us ever set foot on it," Papa said.

Zoe edged around a poison sumac bush. No call to catch the itches.

Maybe it was Hodge's eyes that spooked her. They were too pale for an Indian, almost as light as her own. But his weren't blue. Hodge's eyes were hazel, and bits of amber glinted just below the surface. Folks claimed he got his eye color same way he got his name—passed along by a white granddaddy.

Water had collected in the bottom land, like rain in a barrel. Puddles, big around as wagon wheels, dotted the potato patch. Zoe sank almost to her boot tops in the mud.

"Morning, Mister Hodge," she called across the field.

"Mornin'."

Hodge neither turned nor slowed his methodical digging. That suited Zoe fine. It saved her from making small talk, like "Promising day" or some such nonsense. Any fool could see it wasn't, with rain already beginning to splatter. It was silly to wear a sunbonnet in this weather.

9

She pushed it off. Anyway, her nose was so freckled it looked like she hadn't taken a washrag to it for a month of Sundays.

Perspiration mingled with raindrops and trickled down Zoe's neck as she bent over the tangled vines. Some of the potatoes lay right on top of the ground, easy enough to pick up. Others were half buried, and just as she'd dreaded, she had to poke deep into the sticky earth.

Zoe lost count of how many potatoes she tossed into the basket. Hodge was six or seven rows ahead. That meant she'd have to grub the rest of the day to catch up. As Zoe's hand closed about an especially fat potato, it squirmed. Two bulgy eyes stared up through her fingers.

"Ugh!" Zoe squealed and dropped the toad.

"Hoptoads biting early this season?"

Zoe whirled around. She hadn't heard Hodge approach. He had skimmed right over the muddy ground, silent as a haunt.

"Touch a toad, grow a wart," she retorted, wiping the red clay from her hands on her apron.

Hodge's eyes were as yellow and blank as an owl's, but his mouth twitched ever so slightly. Zoe couldn't tell if he was laughing at her.

"Small wonder I got fooled," she said defiantly. "These potatoes are lumpy as hoppers, and most of them aren't a mite bigger."

"Digging them too soon," Hodge agreed. "But better in your kettle now than in some Yankee stomach later."

"Bluebellies!"

Zoe knew worse names for Yankees, but none she dared to say out loud. At first, when the war began and all the shooting was so far away, Yankees were only bugbears. They were like something she'd made up to threaten Jim Henry into being good. But she was the scaredy one now. Doc Biggs had said a whole swarm of Bluecoats was streaming down along the railroad line from Chattanooga. Every day they got closer, and maybe someday . . .

Goosebumps raised up on Zoe's backbone. Like the warts on a toad! At least she wasn't afraid of one of them. It just gave her a start, that's all. Zoe thrust her fingers deep into the ground and threw another potato into the basket. Mister Hodge had not moved. She could feel his eyes fastened to the top of her head. She wished she hadn't pushed off her bonnet.

It seemed forever before he said, "Found something you might fancy, Miss Snyder."

Zoe looked up. Hodge was holding out his hand.

"It don't bite either."

Now she was certain he'd been funning her before. Zoe straightened and took a small step toward him. In his hand was a bit of tortoise shell, the size and shape of a silver dollar. A hole pierced its center, and it had been polished to a soft gloss.

"Turned it up with the spade," said Hodge. "Reckon this shell's been buried ever since this was Keetoowah land."

"Cherokee," Zoe corrected, and then wished she hadn't. Mister Hodge knew best what to call his kin.

"Back then, when the moon shone full, the villages gathered to dance their prayers. Seems likely right here." Hodge fell silent, looking somewhere over her shoulder at the ridge of hills.

"But how come a tortoise shell?" Zoe persisted.

"Womenfolk wore leg rattles cut from terrapin shells."

"Mama has a tortoise-shell comb," said Zoe.

"For my people, the turtle is a special totem." Hodge reached for Zoe's hand, closing her stiff fingers around the shell. "I reckon you could use a bit of luck."

The tortoise shell felt cool in her hand. "You mean—this is magic? A talisman?"

Hodge smiled, his cheeks crinkling in ridges like a walnut husk. He wasn't even missing a tooth, not a single gap, although Zoe was certain he had long since passed sixty. "Mebbe." Hodge shrugged, his smile fading as quickly as it had appeared. Abruptly, he shouldered the spade and walked away.

"Thank you kindly, Mister Hodge," Zoe called.

She stroked the hard surface of the shell and waltzed partway down the row. She was an Indian maiden dancing beneath a shining moon, a string of turtle shells making music above moccasined feet. Then she skidded, twisting an ankle in the heavy boot. She was just Zoe Snyder again, acting the fool in the potato patch. If Mister Hodge was watching, he'd laugh right out loud.

Zoe went back to the basket. While she'd been lollygagging about, the pile of potatoes seemed to have shrunk. She thrust the tortoise shell deep into her apron pocket. It was better than any charm writ on paper. This token was meant for her. Hadn't Mama called her a tortoise just this morning?

Something fell on the other side of the fence, plopping down on the soft ground. It might be a possum in the corn, but possums did their sneaking after dark. Zoe picked her way through the tangled vines and climbed the splintery rails of the fence.

"Jim Henry!"

Her brother stood shoulder high in the stand of cornstalks. As Zoe watched, he took aim at the scarecrow and a potato sailed through the air.

"Take that, you thievin' Yankee devil!" he yelled.

Jim Henry looked a sight worse than the scarecrow. He wore a torn blue shirt of Papa's that hung down below the knees of his britches. Zoe snickered. "Thief, yourself," she said. "Snitching the taters."

Her brother kicked at a potato. "I'm doing what Mama told me. She said to fetch you up from the field." He stuck out his tongue. "I'm going to tell you took off your bonnet."

"Don't you tell tales on me! You just pick up these taters, every last one."

"Can't. Got to go up to the house. We got visitors."

"Why didn't you say so?"

"I just did. Someone's setting in the parlor, so Mama said—"

"Doc Biggs?" Maybe he'd come to help with the baby.

Jim Henry shook his head. "Go see for yourself."

Zoe grabbed for his arm. "Is it Papa?" Jim Henry

13

dodged and zigzagged through the cornstalks. "Come back here! Get these taters!"

Zoe herself scooped up the scattered potatoes, toting them in the folds of her apron. She climbed over the fence and dumped them back into the basket. Times like this she'd like to take her brother clean apart, from tooth right down to toenail.

"Hodge!" she called across the field. "Mister Hodge! I've got to get up to the house, quick!"

She hitched up her skirts and ran. She didn't care a whit if her stockings showed when she jumped the puddles. She'd only had the tortoise-shell talisman for a few minutes and already her luck was changing!

Saturday

3

When she reached the drive, Zoe stopped short. Her heart, which had hammered in her ears as she ran, dropped like a peach pit into her stomach.

That wasn't Papa's chestnut horse tied to the hitching post. It wasn't Doc Biggs' knobby-kneed mare and shabby buckboard, either. A runabout waited beside the steps to the front veranda. Although the wheels were caked with clay, the dark-green paint was shiny and new, and even from a distance, Zoe could tell the seats were leather. Nowadays, who could drive about in such a fancy fashion? She didn't for a moment think—it couldn't really be—a Yankee who was sitting in their parlor!

Zoe edged cautiously toward the veranda. As she drew closer, she recognized the dapple-gray dozing between the carriage shafts.

"Mrs. Postmaster McFee!" She let out her breath in

an exasperated whistle. Just like that old busybody to come calling when it was near time for dinner.

Zoe trudged to the rear of the house, stomping to shake the soil from her boots before she went in. Mama had conniptions if her carpet got dirty. She tucked a loose strand of hair behind an ear, took off her apron, and hung it from the peg inside the door. The pocket sagged limply. Zoe jammed her hand into it.

"Oh, tarnation!" she cussed under her breath.

The tortoise shell was gone. It was all Jim Henry's fault, getting her so het up she'd forgotten about the shell. "Spoiled as week-old mush, that's what you are," she said loudly. Zoe gave the back door a hearty shove, remembering just in time to catch it before it banged and jarred open the grandfather clock.

The clock stood in the hall, like an oversized sentry guarding the arches to the twin parlors. From Mama's parlor came the murmur of voices. Zoe's boots echoed on the floorboards as she went down the hallway.

"My land! Sounds like the cavalry's coming!"

That was Mrs. McFee's voice, all right. Raspy as chalk on a slate board. Zoe hesitated beneath the arch, reluctant to go in.

Mama's parlor was the show-off room, kept just for company and crowded with treasures that her mother had brought all the way from Atlanta. A flower-strewn Aubusson carpet covered the floor, and a vase of matching sea-blue silk blossoms sat on the marble-top table. But it was the portrait of Grandmother Zoe Stewart that ruled the room. From her gilt frame high over the mantelpiece, Grandmama looked down her nose at everything. Her eyes, wider and brighter than in real life, never seemed to miss a trick.

Mrs. McFee had managed to squeeze herself into the cherrywood rocker. Although a breeze blew through the lace curtains, her face glowed pink beneath her powder and she waved a large ostrich-feather fan. But Zoe's astonished gaze was fastened on someone else: Letitia Jane McFee, perched stiffly on the horsehair sofa.

Letitia Jane's skirts were neatly arranged over hoop and starched petticoats, and her feet were buttoned into soft white kid shoes. Her hair hung in long curls, like bedsprings poking from beneath her bonnet.

You'd think Letty didn't know there was a war on! Zoe's own pigtails were tied with twine. As for petticoats, most of hers were buried deeper than the potatoes. She and Mama had taken the English teapot, the cut-glass pitcher, and the silver knives and forks, wrapped them in Zoe's underskirts, and hidden them root deep beneath the sycamore by the well house.

Letitia looked up and caught Zoe staring. "Why, Zo Snyder!" she called out. "I hardly even recognized you."

"How do, Letty Jane. Afternoon, Missus McFee," Zoe mumbled, stepping through the archway.

"Pleased to see you, Zo." The postmaster's wife saw every inch of Zoe, from the top of her damp head to the heels of Papa's old boots.

Mama sat in the ladder-back chair opposite Mrs. McFee. She wore her polite company smile, but her eyes looked wary as a rabbit's. Mama's fingers nervously creased and then smoothed the edges of an envelope lying in her lap. "You'll have to excuse Zoe's appearance," she said. "She's been helping Mister Hodge get in the early potatoes. We've got to gather them before any Yankees do."

"Hodge?" Mrs. McFee's eyebrows jerked up, brushing the brim of her carriage hat. "That Injun?"

"Mister Hodge is right as rain," Mama replied, "and twice as reliable." She glanced out the window. "My, couldn't we do with some sunshine about now?"

"Couldn't we just?" Mrs. McFee waved her fan more briskly, but she seemed reluctant to change the subject. "Still, an old Injun and a young girl . . ."

"Four hands work faster than two." Mama's tone was crisp. "I've got all I can manage here at the house, and Jim Henry's been frail since the day he was born."

"Pity he don't take after his daddy," the postmaster's wife said, "though your Zo 'pears to favor him."

Another few years and Zoe promised to be nearly as tall as Papa. Already she stood half a head above Mama, and if her feet didn't stop growing, there'd soon be no need to put stuffing in Papa's boots at all. But Mrs. McFee made her feel gawky, like a heron wobbling on long, skinny legs. Zoe shifted from one foot to the other.

"Guess all I got from Mama's side was my name," she allowed, wishing again that Grandmother Zoe Stewart hadn't been so all-fired determined to have a namesake.

Mama sighed. "I cannot settle on what to call the new

18

baby." She patted her lap absently. "But it's a blessed event in these troubled times."

As if in answer, the baby kicked and Mama's ample apron quivered. The unopened letter fluttered to the floor.

Zoe thought she'd like to die, she was that embarrassed. Letitia Jane looked politely at the ceiling, but Mrs. McFee eyed the envelope sharply. Zoe followed her gaze. The stamp bore Jefferson Davis' likeness, with the Confederate postmark carelessly covering one ear. But the handwriting was strange, addressed to Mama in bold block letters.

"Seems to me a name may be the least of your worries," commented Mrs. McFee.

"I do declare!" cried Mama, as if the thought had just occurred. "Haven't we forgot our manners! Zoe, honey, go brew up some tea." She turned to Mrs. McFee and added apologetically, "Sassafrass is all we've got. It's been months since we've had a real tea leaf in the cannister."

The postmaster's wife sighed. "We all must make sacrifices."

"Fetch corn dodgers, too, and some huckleberry preserve."

"Yes, ma'am." Zoe made her escape down the hall, but dainty footsteps tapped after her.

"I'm right anxious to be of help, Zo."

Just like Letty Jane to say her name wrong. But not like Letty at all to want to help. Letty never lent a hand to anyone, at least not when they'd gone to free school together at Spring Place. Zoe hadn't stayed long at that school. Papa had suddenly decided that she could learn to spell and cipher right at home. There'd been mention of sending her to an academy in Atlanta, but the war had put an end to all talk of further schooling. Zoe was just as glad. She'd no doubt but what Atlanta girls would all be cut from the same cloth as Letitia Jane McFee.

"Only takes one to boil up water," Zoe answered shortly.

A pot of chick-peas simmered on the stove for dinner, and Zoe slid the kettle in its place. Letty stood just inside the kitchen door, with her bonnet strings loosened and one small, pink ear resting against the jamb.

Letty smothered a giggle. "Mama never says anything interesting if she knows I'm listening."

Zoe rattled the silver spoons in the drawer. Mama wouldn't bury these. She'd held them back so someone like Mrs. McFee could stir her tea in style.

"Ssssh!" cautioned Letty, but that was hardly necessary. Mrs. McFee's words carried clearly down the hall.

"They say Emma Sanson took a bullet through her skirts, she got that close to Yankee fire."

"How brave!" came Mama's soft murmur.

"Brave? Brazen's more like it. Way I heard, she hopped right up beside General Forrest on his horse."

"And Emma showed him where to ford the creek and surprise the Yankees. Fourteen hundred of them captured, if I'm not mistaken." Mama stopped to catch her breath.

"Well, you'll not catch my Letty gallivanting around like that."

"I'd be right proud if Zoe showed such pluck."

Zoe turned to the steaming kettle and poured the boiling water over the shreds of bark in the cups. Would be nice if there was a concoction you could drink, like a magic potion, that would give a body gumption.

"Can't believe my eyes, the things I see," Mrs. McFee continued. "Just yesterday . . ." She lowered her voice.

Letty's pout made Zoe grin. It was obvious she couldn't catch a word her mother said. Now it was Mama's voice, raised in question, that both girls heard.

"Is it true that Governor Brown's enlisting boys as young as fifteen?"

"That's so. Billy Joe Judson is signed to go before the week is out."

Letitia Jane bore the tray of tea into the parlor, as if she'd truly had a hand in its making instead of an ear at the door. Zoe followed with a plate of cold corn dodgers and a few spoonfuls of last year's huckleberry jam. They'd no sugar to make more this season. As she passed the grandfather clock, she stopped, suspicious. The door was slightly ajar. Zoe jerked it open wide and a small hand waved at her from behind the heavy brass weights.

"Jim Henry!" Zoe hissed. "What in the name of heaven are you doing? You know better than to hide in there."

"Listening," he whispered back. "Same as you and Letty."

"Little pitchers have big ears," warned Zoe, "and you're just begging to have yours boxed. Now, skedaddle!"

Jim Henry snatched a corn dodger as Zoe went past with the plate.

The next half hour dragged so slowly that Zoe wondered if her brother had stopped the clock. The bitter, lukewarm tea made her feel sick. If she so much as sneezed, Mama dosed her with it. Zoe fidgeted in her chair. Letitia Jane was certainly right about one thing. Conversation wasn't nearly so interesting with the two girls in the room.

"A grand digestive, sassafrass," the postmaster's wife affirmed, dabbing at her lips with her handkerchief. Its lace edge was unraveling and dangled in her teacup. "And good for you in your delicate condition, Mrs. Snyder."

"Agreeable," Mama answered.

"You'll leave soon for Atlanta?"

"This is my home, Mrs. McFee. Doctor Biggs looks in when he's up this way, and Zoe can fetch Mrs. Judson when she's needed. Sallie Judson has had six young ones of her own. I daresay she can help bring another into this world."

"Seems a foolish risk to me," Mrs. McFee persisted, "but I suppose you've got good reason." She looked quizzically at Mama over the rim of her cup.

Mama's hand trembled, and tea spilled on her apron. "What a pity!" cried Mama, brushing off the bib. "Shame to waste anything these days. Why, salt's as dear as gold dust and coffee twelve dollars the pound."

Mrs. McFee nodded. "Two hundred dollars, last I heard, for a pair of shoes in Richmond."

The ladies' talk turned from prices to recipes, as if their larders were still full, and to fashions, as if the Union army weren't camped almost upon their doorsteps. Letty Jane yawned loudly and rudely, and Zoe could see her toes wiggling impatiently inside her kidskin shoes. The grandfather clock struck once, and Mrs. McFee snapped open the little watch that hung from a pin on her bodice.

"Half past one!" she exclaimed. "I must get over to the Baptist church and gather up the bandages that the ladies have been rolling."

The postmaster's wife pushed herself up from the rocker. Her eyes darted about the room and then fastened, as if by chance, on the letter still lying on the floor. With an effort, she bent down and picked it up.

"I hope I've brought you good news," she said pointedly, and handed the envelope to Zoe's mother.

Mama slipped the letter into her pocket without a glance and she, too, stood up. "I must not keep you from your errand of mercy," she said.

Mrs. McFee looked annoyed. "Well, we thank you for your hospitality. Come along, Letitia Jane."

Letty jumped to her feet, her face flushed and her eyes bright. Suddenly she was all lit up like Christmas morning. "Leave me here while you tend to your duties, Mother. Please. We girls have hardly had a word together."

23

Zoe was speechless. "How do" was as much as Letitia McFee had bothered to say to her in the past half dozen years.

"If you'll not be a nuisance . . ." Mrs. McFee hesitated.

"No, indeed." Mama glanced out the window. "The rain's let up, so the girls can talk to their hearts' content and pick a basket of huckleberries in the bargain."

"But . . ." Zoe began. She'd never get to find out about the letter with snoopy Letty here. Mama shook her head slightly, and Zoe was aware of some unspoken warning. She changed mid sentence. ". . . But there's potatoes in the basket."

"Use the washtub by the back door. With two of you picking, you might fill it halfway up."

Mrs. McFee swept out beneath the arch like a paddle-wheel riverboat under full steam. "Four-thirty, then, Letitia Jane." She waved her fan. "Mind you behave now, like the young lady you are."

"Trust me, Mama," said Letty. But she caught Zoe's hand as she spoke, and Zoe could feel Letty's crossed fingers pressing against her knuckles.

Saturday
4

Zoe dumped the rainwater that had collected in the bottom of the washtub, picked up a couple of clean flour sacks, and led the way down the lane. Letty followed, lifting her skirts so as not to dirty the ruffles.

This time Zoe turned left off the lane and took the trail toward the well house. Beyond that log building a bramble of huckleberries bordered the creek. The bushes were heavy with ripening berries and so overgrown that the branches hid Hodge's cabin some one hundred yards farther downstream.

But Letty spied the chimney top. "That Injun lives there, don't he?"

Zoe kept on walking. "Most of the time."

"Hodge, Hodge, feathers in his head.
Eats opossum raw with no corn bread!"

Letty chanted behind her back.

Zoe froze. "Don't you say that."

"I can say what I please. Anyhow, you made that rhyme up yourself, if I remember rightly."

Zoe could feel warmth creeping up from her neck to her cheeks. She'd been just as silly then as Jim Henry was now. Worse, maybe. "That was years ago, and I'm sorry I ever did. Papa took me out of free school when he heard me say it. He didn't want that kind of thoughts being put in my head."

"Your daddy's got some funny thoughts of his own." Letty shrugged. "Still has some Northern notions, folks say."

"That's not so!"

"Took his own sweet time enlisting," Letty pointed out.

"He doesn't hold with any killing, that's why," Zoe began, and then thought better of it. There was no explaining Papa's beliefs. "He's got a calling, not a church," Mama said. Mama's own religion came straight from the Episcopalian prayer book, and Zoe wasn't sure she understood that one jot better. She finished, "Your daddy's still to home."

"Being postmaster is very necessary work. Guess you didn't even notice the letter we brought your mama."

"I noticed." Zoe continued down the path.

"Funny. I s'posed you were too busy thinking about that savage you're so friendly with all of a sudden."

If only she dared give Letty a smart kick, right in her flouncy ankles, with one of Papa's heavy boots! Instead

Zoe answered, "I'll mention to Mister Hodge not to scalp you, next time I see him. I reckon he'd rather have a horse's tail hanging from his belt than one of your stiff curls anyhow."

"You're downright spiteful, Zo Snyder, and mean besides, to mention such a thing when my own dear granny got scalped—scalped dead!—by an Injun."

There was a loud sniff and then an uncomfortable silence behind Zoe. She just bet that Letty made that up about her granny, but all the same Zoe wished she could snatch her words back and swallow them. She put down the tub, turned, and held out a flour sack. "Best tie this over that pretty frock," she said by way of apology. "Huckleberries stain bad as walnuts."

"No, thank you," said Letty coolly. "I'm not staying."

"But you told your mother," Zoe began. Look at the trouble her tongue had gotten her into now!

"I told Mama that you and I had scarcely spoken a word. That much is truth and enough for her to know. Now I'm leaving."

"Where?"

"You heard Mama. Billy Joe Judson is off to war. And I'm off to give him a proper good-bye."

"You're never!" Zoe dropped the flour sack. "Billy Joe was the worst tease in school, always knuckling other boys' noses and untying girls' sashes."

"He's grown up now. Most of us have," said Letty sarcastically. "And I'll thank you not to mention this to my mother, or to yours. It's purely my business—and Billy's."

"I don't tattle," Zoe retorted. "You—you're not running off for good?"

"Don't be a goose. I'll be back by four-thirty, and that's probably more than I can say for Mama."

Letty whirled about with a toss of her curls and picked her way gingerly on the wooden planks that spanned the creek. Swollen by the rains, it ran high and red with silt and in places splashed over the bridge.

She'll ruin those shoes! thought Zoe. And how in the world will she manage that hoopskirt in the underbrush?

Zoe didn't start picking huckleberries right away. She went back to the potato patch, retracing her steps of that morning, looking for the tortoise shell. She didn't find it. She knew she wouldn't. Looking for a brown shell in that muddy field was like searching for salt in a sugar bowl.

Hodge was still digging up potatoes. He appeared able to fill the basket as fast without her help as with it. When she called, "Mister Hodge, I'm going berrying, but I'll help you again tomorrow," he merely nodded.

Berry picking was a lonely pastime. Zoe wished Mister Hodge were working closer. Now that she'd got up her nerve to talk to him, she'd like to know more about the shell, about Cherokee magic. For once, she wouldn't have minded Jim Henry's company. Even Letty would have been better than no one. Occasionally something rustled unseen in the prickly bushes. Zoe hoped it wasn't a snake. She hummed loudly to herself, and the berries drummed a tune against the metal sides of the tub. Birds had already gotten some; others were still hard and green.

Zoe wandered farther down the creek bank. Her hands got scratched and stained and her lips turned purple, for every third or fourth huckleberry found its way into her mouth instead of the tub. But hadn't she missed a proper noon dinner, what with the McFees arriving with the letter? If it had been addressed to her, she would have ripped the wrapper open on the spot, right under the nose of the postmaster's wife.

The sun shone fitfully between scudding clouds, and the occasional shadows that the bushes cast on the creek grew longer. It had to be close to half-past four. There was a fair number of berries in the washtub, considering, but she spied neither bonnet nor ruffle of Miss Letitia Jane McFee. Zoe worked her way slowly back toward the plank bridge. As she neared it, Letty approached from the other side. When she got to the middle of the bridge, she stopped so suddenly that she almost catapulted into the creek. Letty, eyes fixed on Zoe, began to scream. It was the most bloodcurdling, hair-raising shriek that Zoe had ever heard.

"Whatever is ailing you, Letty Jane?" Letty's bonnet was askew, but nothing was bruised or broken that Zoe could see.

Letty pointed her finger. "Over—there!"

Zoe wheeled about. A black bear, five hundred pounds if it weighed an ounce, stood no more than ten feet from her in the midst of the huckleberry bushes.

The bear saw Zoe, too. It eyed her warily as the huge

jaws crunched the berries. Perhaps it had been there all afternoon, rustling in the thicket, sharing mouthfuls of berries as the two of them picked, side by side.

The bear rumbled deep in its throat. Letty's howls were making it nervy. Rearing up on hind legs, it struck the air with a forepaw. Mister Hodge claimed a blow from a bear's paw could rip a hound dog apart.

She dared not run; could not even turn her back. Not taking her eyes from the bear, Zoe reached down and picked up a stick. Bears weren't bees. Waving the stick might make matters worse. Instead, she rapped the stick sharply against the tub. It rang like a gong, a jarring, metallic sound. The bear shook its head. Zoe hit the washtub again and again, inching toward the bear. When she was close enough to almost feel the bear's warm breath on her face, Zoe banged the tub so hard she broke the stick.

"Shoo!" she shouted.

For an endless moment, the bear was motionless, as if it had been carved from stone. Then it dropped to all fours and lumbered off through the underbrush.

"Shoo, bear, don't—bother—me," gasped Zoe, but what began as a laugh became a sob. Her knees went soft as mush and refused to hold her up.

Still screaming, Letty crossed the bridge, and Hodge came running from the field. Both of them stood there, looking down at Zoe.

"You're not hurt?" Letty's question was more of a plea.

Zoe shook her head. She couldn't trust herself to speak.

Letty faced Mister Hodge. "You should have seen her!" she cried. "Advancing on that beast like General Lee against the Yankees!"

"Smart." Hodge nodded. "Bears don't like man-made noise, 'specially metal. But Miss Snyder were lucky it was a male. Had it been a she-bear, with young to watch out for, could have ended mighty different."

"You were no help at all," Letty accused. "Why didn't you shoot it?"

"Come too late." The tall Indian bent almost double to whisper in Letty's ear. " 'Sides, I forgot to load my spade."

Zoe choked as swallowed tears met a giggle. Letty Jane had obviously mistaken the spade over Mister Hodge's shoulder for a gun.

Letty flushed. "We'd best go." She put out her hand to help Zoe up, not seeming to mind at all about the berry stains or dirt. "We'll thank you to bring our huckleberries up to the house," Letty told Hodge over her shoulder.

"Yes, miss," he answered politely.

Letty had already turned away, and only Zoe saw him wink. She grinned and bent to pick up the tub of berries.

To hear Letty tell it, her howls scared off the bear. Although she did not come right out and say so, it appeared she'd been on the scene from start to finish, and that was all the story she saw fit to share. Every now and then Mrs. McFee interrupted with a small shriek of her own. Zoe guessed that Letitia came by her screaming naturally, straight from her mother.

"We came close to losing both our little girls!" Mrs. McFee exclaimed.

"I'm not a little girl. I'm fifteen," protested Letty, shaking her head. Her hair wasn't in curls now. The strands that dangled from beneath her bonnet were just as straight as Zoe's own.

I'll wager she puts it up in rags! Zoe wondered how Letty would have explained her appearance to her mother if a bear hadn't happened handily along.

Mrs. McFee blew her nose heartily and the crocheted edging on her handkerchief unraveled even further. "Never for another moment will I let Letitia Jane from my sight."

She looked likely to be as good as her word. Mrs. McFee had her daughter practically sitting in her lap as they drove off in the runabout.

After they'd left, Mama hugged Zoe tight. "Emma Sanson's not the only girl hereabouts who's got pluck," she said.

Saturday
5

Jim Henry had spent the afternoon in the beech tree, "looking out for Yankees" and pelting green nuts at the chickens. He sulked throughout supper, acting as if Zoe had conjured up that bear on purpose, just to leave him out.

"I'd have wrestled that ol' bear, that's what."

"I'll save the next one just for you," said Zoe.

She hoped there'd never ever be another. There was still such a lump in her throat that it was hard to swallow the huckleberries for dessert. She pushed her bowl toward Jim Henry. "You can have my share."

"I reckon," he mumbled through a mouthful of berries, giving Mama a purple grin, "that Zo thinks huckles are *unbearable!*"

Mama shook her spoon at Jim Henry. "Go clean those teeth," she said. "Right now."

That was as near as Mama ever came to scolding him. It wasn't much use, anyhow, for Zoe could hear her brother giggling all the way up the stairs.

After the last dish had been washed and wiped, Mama beckoned to Zoe. "Come with me."

Zoe followed her mother into Papa's parlor. The room smelled of musty papers and rich leather and the faint fragrance of pipe tobacco, slightly sweet, like apples gone soft in the sun. Zoe could almost convince herself that Papa had just stepped out the door for a moment instead of marched off to war.

It was obvious that Mama felt differently. She hugged her arms, shivered, and said, "This room's so empty without your father."

Zoe would hardly call it empty. Her father's room was twin to the company parlor. Both had mortared brick fireplaces and windows opening onto the veranda. But in Mama's parlor everything was in its proper place, while Papa's room was a comfortable clutter. Books of all kinds and sizes spilled from the shelves, and his huge desk was still piled high with ledgers. Zoe's eyes slid automatically to the small volume tied with twine on the third shelf. No one had touched it.

The books had belonged to Papa's own father. Zoe had never known him; her grandfather had died before she was born. But she knew about him. Grandpa had been a Moravian missionary and had come all the way down from Pennsylvania to teach at the Indian school near Spring Place. Poor folks and proud ones alike ad-

34

mired him, but Papa had aimed in a different direction.

"My head is too full of sawdust for preaching or teaching," he had explained to Zoe.

Until the war, Papa had run a sawmill, shipping lumber all over north Georgia. He could whittle most anything and he'd built every inch of their house besides, from digging the cellar to splitting the shingles for the roof. Of course, he'd had to go down to Atlanta for some things, such as hinges for the doors and glass panes for the windows. And one trip, when Papa returned, he brought Mama home as his bride. "Mind you," Papa boasted, "my Mary Alice was such a slip of a gal then that I had to sash her to a keg of nails so's she wouldn't blow right out of the wagon!"

That was hard to picture, looking at her mother now, sitting there at Papa's desk. Mama took the letter from her pocket and held it cautiously, as if it were a powder charge that might explode at any moment. Her hand shook as she picked up the carved ivory letter opener to slit the envelope. The paper tore and she nicked her thumb.

"You've cut yourself!" Zoe exclaimed.

"A scratch," said Mama, and took no notice of the trickle of blood that darkened the ivory handle.

She unfolded the single thin page, and Zoe recognized the handwriting, the smooth, fine script so different from the big block letters on the envelope.

"It's from Papa!"

Mama nodded, her lips moving as she read, silently

tasting each word. Suddenly, she dropped the letter to the desk. "He's coming home!" she cried. "Your father's gotten leave!"

Mama jumped up from the desk and ran to Zoe. What began as a hug ended in a dance as she waltzed Zoe around the room, humming "Sweet Evelina" and stepping in time. Mama was light on her feet, even now, but Zoe felt as clumsy as she had in the potato patch. She had to take care not to trample Mama's skirts with her heavy boots.

"Mama, perhaps you shouldn't—" Zoe warned.

"You're right," Mama agreed breathlessly. "We'll wear the rug through." She collapsed in the chair. "There's so much needs doing! I'll wash the counterpane—perhaps the huckleberries will put up all right in sorghum—and we'll eat the ham! That ham's been hanging in the well house just begging for an occasion!"

"Sounds like Christmas come late!"

"Or early." Her mother's voice turned grave again. "I feared bad news when I saw the envelope, with that strange writing. . . ."

Zoe picked up the letter. It was only the second message from Papa in the seven months he'd been gone.

My Dear Wife,

All is well with me, or as well as may be expected under the circumstances. We have weathered the winter, but still suffer the lack of fresh foodstuffs, and scurvy is rampant. Wounds bleed freely without enough salt in the rations, and with the spring so

wet, mildew grows upon everything. Even the soles
of my boots have rotted through.

Zoe wiggled her toes. She wished she could trade
boots with him now.

There is little I am free to report of my own duties,
other than I am awarded leave. God and the Yankee
pickets willing, I shall get through the enemy lines
safely and be home before the close of June. In time,
I pray, to welcome our child.
With hopes this finds you, our daughter, and son
in good health, I remain your loving husband,
                    John
Postscript: I send this missive by courier to Chat-
tanooga and trust it shall be posted by some loyal
soul from there.

Zoe waved the paper. "No Yankee born could stop
Papa!" she cried.

"Ssssh!" Mama put a finger to her lips. "Not a word
to anyone, not even Jim Henry. The less said of your
father's visit, the safer for him—and for us."

She'd not risk sharing such a secret, not even in her
journal! "I promise," whispered Zoe.

When Mama spoke again, it was to say huskily, "On
no account did I wish Mrs. McFee to know the contents
of this letter, whatever they were."

"You don't mean—surely she's no turncoat!"

"These days, there's no knowing about anyone." Mama
shrugged slightly. "And the postmaster's family doesn't

seem to suffer the same hardships that the rest of us do."

"Mrs. McFee's driving a new buggy!" blurted Zoe, crumpling Papa's letter in her hand. Suddenly aware of what she was doing, she smoothed out the creases and silently gave the note back to her mother.

Mama read it once more, as if memorizing it. But she did not return it to the desk or to her pocket. She held it to the candle flame and, when the edges smoked and curled, threw the letter into the fireplace. Zoe watched it flicker and burn to blend with the other ashes. Both of them started as the grandfather clock struck the hour, its gong echoing down the hall.

"Nine o'clock," counted Mama. She said briskly, "If we bed down before it's fully dark, we'll save on candles." She snuffed the taper, and the smell of warm beeswax hung on the air. Then she closed the damper in the fireplace and pulled the windows shut against the rising wind. Putting her hand on Zoe's shoulder, she shook it gently.

"Go along now, child. There'll be work aplenty to do tomorrow."

That sounded like Mama. For a few minutes her mother had forgot herself and talked to Zoe like the two of them were grown-ups together. "Good night," said Zoe.

Mama went down the hall to her bedroom, and Zoe climbed the steep, wedge-shaped stairs. The rooms above were already in shadow. Zoe glanced apprehensively into the spare bedroom. Within, besides the usual washstand and bed, Mama's wire dress form stood guard over an empty cradle. Zoe could hardly remember the little sister who had slept in the cradle. Just a shock of black hair, like Mama's and Jim Henry's, and kittenlike whimpers in the night. The baby had lived only a few months, taken sick by cholera, and now she slept quietly beneath a small headstone in the cemetery. The cradle awaited another. Zoe hoped it would be a girl.

Jim Henry's door was open, and she could hear the bedsprings twang as he rolled over. Zoe tiptoed past to her own room, last in line, tucked beneath the eaves. There was just enough space for her four-poster bed, carved by Papa from heart oak, a chair, and the low chest beneath the dormer window. The chest did duty as washstand and desk as well. Beside the china basin lay her journal. Zoe inked the pen, cramping her fingers tightly about it so as to squeeze in a few more words beneath the Abracadabra charm.

We had visitors this afternoon. The postmaster's wife, Letitia Jane, and a black bear. All three of them were . . .

Zoe hesitated, and wrote,

DREADFUL!

Too tired to wash, Zoe crawled into bed. But her head refused to stay still on the pillow. Her brain felt close to bursting from thinking.

Papa. Would he be different when he got home? Perhaps he'd had to kill someone.

39

Emma Sanson. Had she been scared, almost eyeball to eyeball with Yankees?

The bear. She could still see it, even with her own eyes shut.

Letty and Billy Joe. They'd spooned. Zoe's mind lingered on the word, thinking of the spoons nested in the drawer of the sink. Letty must have kissed Billy Joe. That notion made Zoe's stomach twitch. Prickles of whiskers had begun to sprout on Billy Joe Judson's cheeks, like the pinfeathers left on a plucked chicken, and he always smelled slightly sour, as if he'd forgotten his Saturday bath. Maybe it was too many huckleberries that made her stomach churn. Maybe that was how Mama felt, with a baby kicking inside.

If you kissed someone, that meant you were as good as engaged, and Letty was but fifteen. Of course, Mama had married Papa when she was only seventeen. She'd left her big, white-pillared house in Atlanta to come upcountry where her nearest neighbor was an Indian.

If Mama had ever felt timid, she never let on. Mama truly had pluck. But it was Zoe, not Mama, that Mister Hodge had given the tortoise-shell talisman to. And she had gone and lost it.

Zoe snuggled under the muslin coverlet. Sheet lightning brightened the sky and silhouetted the topmost branches of the beech tree outside her window. Zoe's eyelids drooped, too heavy to stay open any longer.

Zoe's dreams were twisted together, as confusing as her thoughts. She was dancing again. She twirled about, light as a winged maple seed, and tortoise-shell rattles jingled at her ankles. Then, somehow, Billy Joe Judson was dancing, too, holding her tight in his arms. Zoe pushed at him, but he squeezed harder, and Zoe realized that Billy was really a bear. She broke and ran, with Billy Joe Bear in pursuit, through the woods, across the creek, up the lane, and into the house. Zoe slammed and bolted the door. The door to the grandfather clock swung ajar and she peeked within. Peering back were two pop eyes. A toad croaked, "Zo-eee! Zo-eee!"

"Zoe!"

She forced her eyes open. Like something from her nightmare, what seemed to be a ghost trembled in the doorway. Jim Henry, in trailing white nightshirt and toting his pillow, tiptoed to her bedside.

"Zoe, I can't sleep with so much noise."

"Just thunder. Say your prayers and pull your covers over your head."

"I want to stay here."

Zoe was too sleepy to argue. She dragged the trundle cot from under her bed, and Jim Henry curled up on it, fast asleep before she'd even covered him with one of her quilts. Outside, the wind lessened and the lightning faded. But with the coming of day, the thunder began again, booming loud and close. Zoe Snyder, deep in dreams, paid it no heed.

Sunday
6

It was the cock's crow that woke her. The rusty voice of Jim Henry's rooster challenged the sun as it struggled through shreds of smoky clouds. Angel. A silly name for such a boastful, bad-tempered old bird. Papa had been Bible reading one Sunday and telling about the winged angel of the Lord. Jim Henry had been certain that a winged angel was a rooster.

Angel must have wakened Jim Henry this morning, too, for the trundle cot beside Zoe's bed was empty. The smell of fried mush drifted up the stairwell. That meant there was something special about this Sunday. Zoe poured some water from the pitcher into the basin, splashed her face, and dressed quickly.

Jim Henry was perched on a stool at the kitchen table, wearing his shoes but still in his nightshirt. Seated beside him was Mister Hodge. Zoe stared. Hodge had donned a gentleman's ruffled shirt, with a stickpin at the collar, a vest, and a rusty black frock coat, the kind usually saved for funerals. Atop his head was a tall stovepipe hat. Whatever would Letty McFee—or her mother—make of Mister Hodge here and now? Hodge caught her eye, nodded, and poured molasses on his mush. Jim Henry did the same.

"Mister Hodge has come to bid good-bye," Mama said briefly. "He's going away."

Zoe rubbed the crumbs of sleep from her eyes. "Away?"

"For a spell," Hodge answered.

Mama turned from the stove. "He says a Union force is but a few miles distant. It's not safe for him to stay. The Yankees might impress—or imprison—him."

"The thunder . . ." Zoe wondered aloud.

"Cannon," said Hodge. "Skirmishes."

"They might come here—soldiers?" asked Zoe. "To our own house?"

"A scout party's headed down the road. This'n is the soundest homestead hereabouts, and Yankees don't take second best."

"I won't let any Yankee in," Jim Henry declared. "I'll guard the door."

Hodge put down his fork. "Safer to receive them"— he cast a sidewise glance at Jim Henry—"and not rile them." Then he looked directly at Zoe. "It may be help will come some other way."

Zoe looked down at the floor. He meant the tortoise-shell talisman, of course. She could not tell him she'd already lost it.

43

Hodge shoved back from the table. "My cabin is yours, if needed."

Mama clasped his large hand in her two small ones. "You've helped so much already, Mister Hodge. I do wish I could pay you. John gets but eighteen dollars a month for soldiering, and even that is seldom received. . . ."

"It was his own father that taught me to read and cipher." Hodge touched his finger to his hat brim. "I am the one who owes a debt."

Zoe wished, suddenly and strongly, that he would stay. But Mister Hodge shouldered his muzzle-loader and closed the door silently behind him. Only the spade, propped against the wall, and the full basket of potatoes gave evidence of his surprising visit.

Zoe sat down beside Jim Henry. She wasn't hungry, but she supposed she had better eat while she could. Her brother ran his finger around the rim of his plate, mopping up the last dribble of molasses. No place was set for Mama. She must have eaten already, or given her share to Mister Hodge. By the looks of things, she'd been up since daybreak. The counterpane was in the washtub, rinsed and waiting to be hung, and the ham sat on the dry sink. Zoe bolted her breakfast.

"What should I do first?" she asked her mother.

"To begin, we've got to hide what food we can. Folks claim a troop of Bluecoats can chew up vittles faster than a swarm of locusts. Jim Henry, trot the cornmeal and the huckleberries down to Mister Hodge's cabin."

44

"All by myself?" Jim Henry seemed to have lost his daring during the night.

"Just step smart, like a Johnny Reb," Zoe encouraged him. "Left, right, left, right, all the way there and back."

Jim Henry looked down at his feet. "I forget which one is right and which one is left over."

"Right's on the same side as your right hand. The one you've been licking molasses from."

"Yes, sir!" Jim Henry slid off the stool and snapped his heels together. He marched out the door, swinging a sack of cornmeal in one hand and a pail of huckleberries in the other.

Zoe could hear him chanting, "Left, right!" as he rounded the house. She grinned at her mother, but Mama's eyes had filled with tears. She rubbed the tips of her fingers against her forehead, as if she could erase the worries from her mind.

"I hope I'm doing the right thing, keeping us here. Jim Henry's hardly more than a baby, and two women alone . . ."

Two women! Zoe straightened her shoulders.

"I suppose we'll be safer hid away in Hodge's cabin," her mother went on, "but we'll not get the chance to take much with us. We mustn't be caught carrying the ham, and there are all those potatoes. And we've no time at all to bury the spoons with the other silver."

Zoe eyed the ham, still wrapped in a sack and tied with string, as it had hung in the well house. "We'll—

we'll hide the ham inside your dress form that's up in the spare bedroom. We can pull a frock right over it."

Mama looked startled for a moment, then she giggled and said, "I reckon not even a Yankee would be rude enough to peek beneath a lady's skirt!" She handed Zoe the ham. "Best look about while you're up there and fetch any clothes you and Jim Henry might be needing."

Zoe cradled the ham in her arms as if it were a baby. "As for the taters and the spoons, I'll think on them."

Her words sounded brave enough, but what she was truly thinking was fearsome. What if the Yankees were here when Papa came? If they might lock up Mister Hodge, what could happen to a Rebel soldier? Zoe climbed the stairs quickly so that Mama would not notice how she blinked back the smarting in her own eyes.

The ham swung within the dress form like some strange beast in a wire cage. Zoe slipped her own sprigged-muslin frock over it. It hung like a meal sack, for the form had been made to fit her mother as a bride, but she sashed in the extra folds. Next she went to Jim Henry's room, where she gathered up three shirts, trousers, and his underdrawers. From her own chest she chose an overskirt, two shirtwaists, stockings, and the last of her petticoats. There was nothing in her room worth hiding, save her journal. It lay open on her chest as she had left it last night. Zoe quickly flipped the page. Dipping the pen, she wrote:

46

The enemy is coming.

Sunday, June 19, 1864

Then she pushed the book beneath her mattress, scooped up the garments, and marched resolutely down the stairs to the kitchen. She hesitated at the door, uncertain where to put the armload of clothing. The basket of potatoes still sat by the door.

"Jehoshaphat!"

Zoe dumped the clothes on the sink board and took the clean counterpane from the washtub. She carried it dripping across the kitchen and out into the yard. There she draped it from a low branch of the hawthorn tree that shaded Mama's bedroom window. Back in the kitchen, she wiped out the tub and piled the clothes within, except for her own petticoat. This she tucked tidily over the potatoes in the basket. To any observer, two containers of clothing awaited pickup by their owners.

"Mama?"

"In here."

Her mother's voice came from Papa's parlor. Mama had already cleared the desk, save for the letter opener and a bill or two. Now she was pulling books from the shelves.

"I'm hiding your father's accounts in the pages of his books. Soldiers won't snoop there. Most can't even read, I'll wager." She selected the string-tied volume from the third shelf.

"Not that one, Mama! Please."

"Whyever not?" Mama read aloud, "*Proverbs, Maxims, and Curious Folk Beliefs.* I cannot imagine . . ." She stopped. "Is this where you get that fiddle-de-dee you're always spouting?"

Zoe nodded. Most of Papa's books were as dry as the dust on their covers. But this one had caught her fancy as soon as she'd read the title. It had been even better than she'd hoped—page after page of magic charms and sayings.

"Flapdoodle!" Mama's disgust was clear, but she returned the book to the shelf. "Well, you will have more important matters to dwell on now, that's certain." She took down a Greek grammar and tucked a bill of lading between its covers.

"There's something else," Mama murmured, picking up the letter opener and walking to the fireplace. Slowly she counted the bricks, ". . . Four . . . five . . . six . . . seven."

The seventh brick down from the mantelpiece looked no different from the others, but, as Zoe watched, her mother worked the letter opener into a slight crack in the mortar. Wriggling it gently, Mama slipped the brick from its place. "Look."

The brick had been molded only half as thick as the rest. The space behind it was like a secret cupboard. Zoe caught her breath. Hidden treasures! Perhaps Papa had put away gold dollars before the mint at Dahlonega had closed. Or maybe the pearl-and-garnet brooch that

48

Grandmother Stewart wore in her portrait now lay concealed in that cubbyhole. She crowded Mama, looking over her shoulder.

Papers. The crevice was stuffed with more dusty old papers. Zoe felt betrayed. "Is that all?"

"It's enough," Mama said sharply. "Christening records. The land deed, and . . ." She pulled off her narrow gold wedding band and tucked it beside the yellowing documents. Then she fitted the brick back into place. "Just so you know," said Mama. "The chimney will stand come fire—or whatever."

The two went silently back to the kitchen. There was no need to talk about *whatever*.

Mama managed a smile when she saw the clothes and realized what was hidden beneath Zoe's petticoat. "That sets my own head to working," she declared.

She got needle and thread from her bedroom and the silver spoons from the drawer of the dry sink. Then she knelt awkwardly on the floor beside Zoe. "Don't move," she instructed.

With quick, long basting stitches she turned up the hem on Zoe's skirt, working spoons into the fold as she went. Zoe stood stiff as the dress form, jerking only once when the needle stuck her leg. The skirt was full and, although the heavy silver made it dip unevenly above Zoe's boots, a dozen spoons got sewn into its hem. Mama had just bitten off the thread when Jim Henry burst into the kitchen.

"Yankees! They're marching up the lane! And Zoe, you were right. One really is a devil, 'cause he's got red hair!"

Jim Henry dived under the table. A minute later, the knocker fell heavily against the front door.

Sunday

7

Jim Henry stayed under the kitchen table, but Zoe followed her mother down the hall. Although Mama's face was pale, her step was steady. Zoe walked with caution, for unless she placed one foot directly in front of the other, the spoons slipped and clanked.

Mama drew back the bolt and opened the heavy front door. On the veranda stood a Union captain in full parade dress. A waxed mustache decorated his upper lip, and brass buttons festooned his bright-blue coat. A pistol was buckled in his belt, and a sword hung in its scabbard down his left leg, brushing his shiny black boots. Even so, Zoe found something disturbingly familiar about him. Perhaps it was because his uniform made him look like one of Jim Henry's lead soldiers, before the paint had chipped away.

At the sight of Mrs. Snyder, the captain doffed his

broad-brimmed hat. The top of his head was but an inch or two above Zoe's own, and as bald as a bed knob. She knew now what he reminded her of, with his skimpy hair and naked ears, his close-set eyes and pointy nose poking out above his mustache. A possum. A stupid, sneaky, nighttime-prowling varmint.

"Good morning, ma'am. Captain Benjamin Hetcher of the Ohio Ninety-Third. We'll be partaking of your hospitality."

"Hospitality?" Mama's voice would have frostbit a pumpkin.

"Bed and board, if you prefer. A privilege I'm sure you are happy to grant the United States Army."

Zoe looked over Mama's shoulder at the men milling about the front yard. There must be a score of them, not taking mules and horses into account.

"It is not possible for me to put up your army," Mama replied, "or even that portion of them who have already trampled my garden. I have not room, nor stores enough to provision."

The captain pushed his boot inside the door. "My men will find their own food. As for space, only myself, my sergeant major, and my aide will quarter in your home. Morton! Boone!"

A giant of a man, as red-haired and red-bearded as Sherman himself, clumped up the veranda steps. The boards creaked in complaint beneath his feet.

Zoe gasped out loud. Jim Henry's devil!

A tall, lanky youth followed. He wore an old shirt and trousers and looked more fitted out for haying than

52

for fighting. His hair was hay-colored, too, and when he saw Zoe inspecting him, he smiled. She scowled in return and ducked inside the parlor archway.

Mama stepped back as well. "It appears I have little choice in the matter," she said.

The three Yankees, captain in the lead, walked into the company parlor. Their muddy feet left ugly brown stains on the blue Aubusson carpet. The red-haired sergeant didn't notice, and the captain obviously didn't care. The younger man blushed pink to the roots of his yellow hair when he saw the dismay on Mama's face, and he went back to scrape his heels against the veranda steps.

Captain Hetcher looked about and nodded his approval. To the sergeant major he said, "This will do." Then he added to Mama, "I'll take my meals here. Dinner at noon, supper at six."

He crossed the hall to Papa's parlor. The others waited beneath the arch. "Your husband's study, ma'am?"

"My husband is not at home," Mama replied.

The captain smirked. "It would appear he was about some months ago."

Zoe sucked in her breath. Surely Mama would not abide such rudeness. But Mama just stood stiff as a broom, without a word, as if it were beneath her dignity to answer.

Captain Hetcher was unabashed. He drew his sword and tapped it against the desk. "Made to order for me and my work."

Still swinging the sword, he strutted down the hallway. The sergeant, the aide, Mama, and Zoe followed like hens after a bantam rooster. The captain stopped in front of the grandfather clock.

"Biggest damn timepiece I ever saw," he muttered. "Looks more like a coffin than a clock." He pulled a large gold watch from his pocket. "It's running three minutes slow as well. Still, there's firewood in it aplenty to take the chill off my bones." The captain coughed and then complained, "I've not seen enough blue sky in Georgia to make a pair of Dutchman's breeches."

Burn the clock! No other grandfather clock was ever so tall or so wide, and a Cherokee rose twined its way up the side. The works had been specially made, across the ocean in Germany, and Papa had carved the walnut case himself. The clock was to be part of Zoe's dowry when she married. "Or when you're tall enough to wind it, whichever comes first," Papa had teased. She'd been able to reach the key since she had turned twelve, and already the top of her head was crowding six-thirty.

No way Zoe could hold her temper now. That would be harder than holding back the steam in a boiling kettle. She planted herself firmly before the clock. That Yankee would have to cut her into little pieces before she'd let him harm it. "No!"

The captain eyed her, twitching up one brow and at the same time curling his lip down beneath his mustache. Then he shrugged and led the parade on down the hall.

Reluctantly, Zoe followed them into Mama and Papa's

54

bedroom. Captain Hetcher was staring out the bay window, gazing out at the yard and the hawthorn tree. Colored glass, shipped from Philadelphia, bordered the window. When the sun shone through, patches of color, like pieces from a crazy quilt, danced upon the floor. The sun wasn't shining now, and the only thing that danced was the coverlet that Zoe had hung from the tree. It twisted in the breeze and occasionally slapped against the glass.

"What's that? A shroud?" Captain Hetcher asked sourly.

Zoe shivered. Coffins and shrouds. Captain Hetcher was possessed by a mighty morbid mind.

"The counterpane for the bed," Mama answered. "I washed it this morning."

"So I was expected!" The captain chuckled. "How thoughtful." He pushed a finger into the feather bed. "Sweet dreams! I shall sleep here." He made a half bow. "With your permission, ladies."

"With your permission, sir," Mama said icily, "we shall sleep in the Indian cabin down by the creek."

"Injun!" Captain Hetcher wheeled about. "Didn't know there were any redskins in these parts."

"There aren't any—now," Mama replied.

The captain's breath hissed through his teeth in a wheeze of relief. "Stay where you will, then, but make certain that no one leaves this property at any time." He turned to his sergeant. "You and Boone lodge upstairs."

"There's room for Walker, too," the man named Morton answered. "He's been shaking with fever this past week and—"

"No!" Captain Hetcher interrupted. "I won't have any sickness under this roof. Besides, I want only three of us. Three's my lucky number."

He swaggered into the kitchen, curling his finger at Zoe to follow. "You look healthy enough. You'll do the serving up and chores, eh, miss?" Zoe looked down at her feet. "Cat got your tongue? No matter." He turned to Mama. "I fancy coffee with my breakfast."

"There is no coffee. We make do with a brew of parched chestnuts."

Captain Hetcher grimaced. "Biscuits . . ."

"We've neither salt nor flour."

"Boone!" The boy jumped. "Fetch the missus some flour and a five-pound bag of rock salt."

"Yes, sir!"

The aide saluted and went out, slamming the door. Zoe could hear the creak as the clock case swung open on its hinges.

"Perhaps an egg or two," the captain continued, "and a chicken for my Sunday supper."

"You can hardly have both, Captain," Mama said mildly. "I've but two hens left. Eat them and you'll get no eggs."

"Kill that scrawny rooster out front. He looks overdue for the skillet." Captain Hetcher smiled broadly, showing such snow-white teeth that Zoe wondered if they were store-bought. "The way I hear it, southern womenfolk are famous for their fricassee chicken."

A howl came from beneath the kitchen table. Startled, the captain ordered the sergeant, "See what bird crows like *that*, Morton!"

The large man stooped, reached beneath the table-cloth, and pulled out Jim Henry by an arm and a leg. Jim Henry sank his teeth into the sergeant's wrist.

"Ow!" grunted Morton, loosening his grip.

"Not Angel!" yelled Jim Henry as he ducked behind Zoe.

"Not angel is right," the sergeant mumbled and rubbed his wrist. "Bites more like a hornet."

Zoe hugged Jim Henry against her back. "Angel's the name my brother gave the rooster."

"A chicken!" The captain chuckled and patted his waistcoat buttons. "Well, that angel's going to taste right heavenly!"

Jim Henry darted out from behind Zoe and aimed two furious fists at Captain Hetcher's stomach. Zoe snatched her brother by the tail of his nightshirt and jerked him back. Her skirt swung about her boot tops, and a spoon slipped from its hem.

"Please, no, please," prayed Zoe under her breath, trying to put her foot over the spoon.

But the captain's hand was quicker. "Coin silver!" he declared, weighing the spoon in his fingers.

Captain Hetcher snared Zoe's skirt with the tip of his sword. Another spoon clattered to the floor. Zoe bit her tongue to keep from hollering in front of everyone.

"I've always hankered to spoon my soup with gen-

57

uine silver. But perhaps you yourself would prefer to remove any other tableware stitched in your skirt."

Tight-lipped, Mama nodded at her. Zoe's fingers trembled as she broke the threads and one by one withdrew the spoons.

". . . Ten . . . eleven . . . twelve," Captain Hetcher counted, lining up the spoons on the table. Then he looked at Mama and tugged throughtfully on his mustache. "I wonder . . ."

Zoe gasped. He would not dare to search Mama! He could not doubt that was a real baby swelling beneath her apron. This time it was Zoe who clenched her fists, but it was Mama's cold stare that made the captain avert his eyes. He glanced sharply at Jim Henry instead.

"Sergeant! Find out if this little thundercloud has a silver lining."

Morton picked up Jim Henry cautiously, holding him at arm's length.

"Don't eat me!" cried Jim Henry.

"*Eat* you?" The sergeant guffawed. "There'd be more meat on a mosquito." He flipped Jim Henry upside down. The nightshirt flew over his head, but no silverware fell out. Jim Henry blushed redder than his rooster.

"Pity," murmured the captain, "but perhaps there's something else I've overlooked."

Using his sword, he pried open cupboards, lifted the lids of storage bins, and poked in the ashes of the firebox in the stove. He even upended the rain barrel that stood on the kitchen stoop.

White-knuckled, Mama braced herself against the dry

sink. Zoe tried to look equally brave, standing as straight and still as she could, willing her knees not to shake. Behind her back she hid Mister Hodge's spade and gripped the handle hard.

Captain Hetcher frowned down at the washtub and the basket, both brimful of clothes, "Seems a peculiar amount of washing for a ma and two young'uns," he commented.

"We're taking such clothing as needed down to the cabin," Mama retorted.

"Enough here for a fancy dress ball," the captain continued. He flung aside the petticoat folded on top of the basket. "Ha!" He neatly speared a potato with his sword and smiled smugly at the silent watchers. "Potatoes go nicely with chicken."

He advanced on the washtub. "Maybe you have the dessert in this one." He flipped it over with his boot, and shirtwaists, trousers, underclothes, and stockings tumbled on the floor. The captain looked sheepish.

"I've got more important things to do than play hide-and-seek," he muttered. He turned to Mama. "I advise better cooperation during our stay here, madam."

"And how long will that be, Captain?"

"You'll have the honor of our company as long as it pleases me. A fortnight is possible."

Zoe piled the clothes into the washtub once again, burying her face in the starched petticoat. Two weeks! Anything could happen in a fortnight. Papa could come home. The whole world might come to an end.

Sunday
8

Yankees had sprung up everywhere, like toadstools after the rain.

The lane was a muddle of mules and men. Some soldiers washed their clothes down at the well house. Others scrubbed in the creek, ducking one another, acting as silly as Jim Henry. A few shuffled cards, gambling and cussing, right on the front veranda.

Even the indoor air was cloudy, for Captain Hetcher took his ease in the company parlor, smoking a twisted black cigar. His feet were propped on the marble-top table, and he tapped his ashes into the vase with the blue silk flowers. Morton, the big redheaded sergeant, thundered up and down the stairs, moving his gear into the spare bedroom. The ceiling shook with every step, and Zoe was certain the plaster would come tumbling down. Poor Mama! She'd been so prideful of her house, and already it had begun to look bad as a pig wallow.

Zoe did her best to ignore everyone and everything. She helped Mama gather their bedding together to take down to Hodge's cabin. The young aide with the light hair sprang to his feet when he saw her.

"May I tote that for you, sis?" he asked.

Sis! "I'll thank you to tend to your own concerns," Zoe retorted. But she was unable to handle the heavy door with the armload of quilts, and she had to let him hold it open for her.

Yankees stared at her as she went down the lane. Eyes down, Zoe did not glance at any of the intruders except for a young hound dog, all ears and ribs. A stray.

"Are you Reb or Yankee?" Zoe asked. It looked up at her and wagged its tail, but she shook her head regretfully. "No food to spare where I'm headed," she said.

Jim Henry was already at the cabin. Although she'd not have the heart to do it, Mama had threatened a licking if he so much as poked his nose out the door. He sat morosely on the only chair.

Zoe had never set foot in Mister Hodge's cabin before, never had cause to. It was but one room, and that not much over twelve feet square. A bed was wedged in one corner, a table in another, and a bearskin rug stretched before the fireplace. The walls were rough logs, chinked with red clay, and broken only by a small window, with oiled paper panes to let in the light. Nothing personal marked the man who'd lived here, not even a mirror. How would a person know who he was if he couldn't see himself now and then? Still, the cabin was dry and had been swept clean. No spiderwebs hung from the rafters, and there was a pattern of fresh broom tracks on the dirt floor.

Zoe dumped the quilts on the bed. "I suppose this will do for Mama." She eyed the sagging, straw-stuffed tick doubtfully.

"How 'bout us?" asked Jim Henry. "Where do we sleep?"

"On the floor." Jim Henry's lower lip quivered, so Zoe added brightly, "We'll be like honest-to-goodness Graycoats camping out!"

"Can I sleep atop that bear?"

" 'Deed you can," Zoe promised. Nothing under the sun could make her put her head down on a bear-skin.

Jim Henry squinted at the single pot hook hanging in the fireplace. "How we going to eat?"

"We'll have walk-down suppers. I'll fetch things from the house."

"I'm hungry now."

"You just be good here for a little bit more. I've got to help Mama. There's a basket of corncobs for you to play with."

"Corncobs don't do nothing."

Zoe considered for a moment. "You can pretend they're soldiers. I'll be back sooner than you think."

Sooner became later. Captain Hetcher kept Zoe busy at chores, even rinsing out his black silk hose. Then she'd helped to fix his dinner, thickening the drippings while Mama sliced the chicken.

"Best I could do," said Mama as she sawed at the rooster with the knife. "This poor old bird could cook all week and never get tender."

"Serves him right, eating Angel. Maybe he'll break his store teeth," answered Zoe, and might have said more had not the captain suddenly appeared in the doorway.

"That clock of yours struck six ten minutes ago," he complained in a whiney, up-north twang. Zoe hated the sound of his voice almost as much as his looks.

"I'm dishing up supper now," Mama said, handing the platter to Zoe.

Zoe, eyes upon the plate, had scarcely moved a foot across the floor when she collided head-on with Captain Hetcher. Chicken gravy dribbled down his shiny boots.

"Clumsy!" Hetcher barked.

It was not her fault, and Zoe almost said so. For no good reason he'd stepped into the kitchen, directly into her path. She wiped his boot with the hem of her skirt. The captain ignored her, staring above her head at something else.

"What's that spade doing there?"

"Doing what it's been doing all day," Mama snapped, "leaning against the wall."

"Get rid of it!" the captain demanded shrilly. "It's bad luck."

Mama raised a quizzical eyebrow. "Do tell," she said. Despite the pertness in her voice, her step was slow and tired as she moved to put the spade outside the kitchen door.

Captain Hetcher shuddered. "A spade in the house means a grave to be dug."

Zoe steadied the platter in her hands. She knew that superstition, too. But maybe they need not be fearful. If a grave was to be dug, it might be for Captain Hetcher.

The last light was leaving the sky when Zoe returned to the cabin. Jim Henry waited at the door. His eyes were red and puffy.

"I thought Captain Itcher got you!" he wailed.

"Hetcher," Zoe corrected, "and I got him, in a manner of speaking. Look." She uncovered the kettle she'd brought. "Mama held back the neck and giblets for us, and there's grits with gravy and some butter beans besides."

"I want Mama, too."

"She'll be down in a wink. She's sent you something else."

Jim Henry brightened. "Sweet potato pie!"

"Now where on earth would she get pie?" Zoe reached in her pocket. "The pulleybone."

Jim Henry's face fell again. "Angel?"

Zoe nodded.

Jim Henry sighed, but he didn't cry. He grasped one end of the wishbone while Zoe held the other. "Wish," he commanded, "then pull."

They tugged at the bone, but it only bent beneath their fingers like a green willow twig. Zoe braced her thumb against it and yanked. Reluctantly, the bone broke.

"I won! I got the long end!" Jim Henry waved his half of the wishbone in the air. "I wished I still had Angel."

"Well, that wish will come true, sure enough. One of the hens has hidden a nest, and there's certain to be an Angel among the chicks."

"How can I know?"

"You can't, at first, but after a bit one of them will grow a topknot on his head and be sassier than the others."

"Then I'll call him Rebel!"

Zoe smiled. "You do that."

"What about your wish, Zo?"

"You're not supposed to tell, but I reckon it doesn't matter. I wished the Yankees would go away."

Jim Henry puffed up. "We'll scare them off, you, and me, and Rebel!"

"They're not likely to be frightened of us."

"I could roll in the poison sumac. When I break out all over, you could say it was the spotted fever."

Zoe looked at her brother with admiration. "That's downright clever, but it would take too long. We need to be rid of them soon." *Before Papa comes,* she added to herself.

Both of them stared silently across the fields. Campfires flickered as the Yankees dried their clothes and cooked their suppers. Most of the fires were in the cornfield. Probably roasting green ears, Zoe guessed. If they got the colic, then Mama would have to dose them all with sassafras tea.

"Moon's rising," said Jim Henry.

"Got a ring around it," answered Zoe. "Sure sign of bad weather."

A lonely flame flared up by the well house. Zoe studied it anxiously. It appeared to be kindled close to the bushes where she and Mama had buried the crystal and silver. At least a bonfire kept berry-picking bears away.

Some soldier had a fiddle, and the sweet-sad notes of "Home, Sweet Home" rose with the smoke on the damp evening air.

"Kind of pretty, isn't it?" asked Jim Henry. "Looks like lightning bugs in the field."

Zoe snorted. "Those are our fence rails they're burning. Come on." She took her brother by the hand. "We'll light the corncobs and make a campfire of our own in the fireplace while we're waiting for Mama."

"I'll get the cobs!" Jim Henry darted ahead into the cabin. "These are my armies," he explained, pointing to the corncobs laid out on the floor in two opposing rows. "Here's the South, and this is the North." He grabbed up an armful of the latter. "Let's fire up these Damnyankees first!"

Monday
9

Something—some noise—made Zoe open her eyes. The windowpanes were no brighter than pale gray squares, so it was not long past daybreak. She lay rigid on the floor, listening. A tree creaked in the wind, and a squirrel, or another creature, scampered across the roof. She could hear the straw mattress rustle as her mother turned and a slight whistling snore from Jim Henry, curled on the bearskin rug. Otherwise, all was quiet. Then a rifle shot split the silence.

"Mama?" she whispered.

Her mother shifted, but her breathing was still deep and regular. Zoe buried her face in her pillow. If it was a battle beginning, she did not want to see it, or hear it. But who could the Yankees be shooting at? No Johnny Rebs hereabouts, excepting the Home Guard like old Uncle Willis. Or some stray soldier. Like Papa.

Zoe threw off the quilt and pushed to her feet. She was stiff from spending the night with only a reed pallet between her and the hard-packed dirt floor, and her dress was wrinkled from tossing in her sleep. Zoe smoothed down her hair, not even trying to part or plait it without a mirror, and pulled on her boots. She tiptoed to the door.

Wisps of nighttime mist drifted over the fields. Thunderheads held promise of showers to come, but dawn had lined each cloud with pink. Zoe sniffed. Even the air smelled fresh and sweet at this hour of the morning. Usually she stayed abed until much later, till Mama had called her twice at least.

A rifle cracked in the cornfield and Zoe jumped. The scarecrow's hat flew through the air, and a flock of crows flapped and cawed their protests. Other shots, at spaced intervals, seemed to come from up by the house. Zoe hurried in that direction.

Half a dozen Yankees stood no more than seventy-five yards from the house. They were lined up in a row, just like Jim Henry had arranged the corncobs. One by one, each raised his gun and took aim at the weather vane that topped the gable. The iron horse that usually trotted so bravely in the breeze whirled dizzily as the bullets hit and ricocheted. The arrow that supported its flying hooves was bent down toward the ground.

Zoe ducked behind the honeysuckle, too riled up to be scared of the bees. These cotton-headed soldiers were playing games! Ruining the weather vane, spoiling a beautiful morning and all the mornings yet to come! She was too angry to be scared of the Yankees, either.

"You all stop that right now, hear?" she shouted.

As one man, the soldiers lowered their guns and stood at attention. Zoe was thunderstruck. She'd never for a moment believed they'd heed her. When she poked her head from the bush, she realized that they were looking beyond her. Captain Hetcher was standing on the veranda.

He was in his stocking feet, with suspenders pulled up over his undershirt. He'd not yet waxed his mustache, and it drooped like skinny little mouse tails on either side of his mouth. Sergeant Morton, fully dressed, leaned against the front doorjamb.

"What in tunket's going on?" bellowed Captain Hetcher. "Wasting bullets! Behaving like schoolboys!"

"We're just practicing, Captain," one soldier apologized.

"I'll practice you! I've better ways to keep you busy. This is war, not some shooting match! Report to me within the hour."

"Yes, sir, Captain, sir." The six men saluted and then scattered like buckshot.

Captain Hetcher watched their departure, scowling. Then his glance fell on Zoe, still half hidden by the honeysuckle. "You're up early, miss."

"I couldn't sleep."

"You're not alone in that complaint. That tough bird you served up gave me indigestion. Might as well have eaten my boot instead." He glared at her with red-rimmed eyes. "It was already covered with gravy."

"Should I fix breakfast?" Zoe asked.

"Nothing." The captain did indeed look ill. "Just coffee. In the library."

It was a moment before Zoe realized that he meant Papa's parlor. She started to follow Captain Hetcher, but Sergeant Morton blocked the doorway.

"Now me," said Morton, "I'm hungry as a horse. Dreamed over and again about ham. It was so real I swear I could smell it!"

"Imagine that!" Zoe ducked under the sergeant's arm. "You might as well forget about ham or anything else," she added over her shoulder. "Captain's orders were to cook for him. I heard nary a word about having to fix for others!"

In the kitchen, Zoe began to tremble. She could not keep her hands from shaking as she measured the ground chestnuts into the water. Whatever had gotten into her, back talking like that? That wasn't Emma Sanson's kind of pluck when she'd stood up to the Yankees. It was Zoe Snyder's pure pigheadedness.

The brew from the roasted chestnuts, thin and slightly red, looked more like creek water than coffee. But Zoe poured a steaming cupful and, head down, bore it through the hall and into Papa's parlor.

Captain Hetcher leaned back in Papa's chair and cleaned his fingernails with Papa's letter opener. Zoe put the cup down abruptly.

"I've taken a fancy to this letter opener," the captain said. "Genuine ivory." He frowned at the spots on the handle. "Dirty."

"That's blood," answered Zoe, remembering Mama's nicked finger.

The letter opener clattered to the desk. "Wash it!" Captain Hetcher ordered hoarsely. Zoe slipped it in her pocket.

The captain eyed the mock coffee with suspicion. He sniffed the cup, then took a sip. Face flushing, he spat it back in the saucer. "If I wasn't feeling poorly already, this would surely do it." He tried another swallow. "Mis-sis-*sip*-pi!"

Zoe backed toward the hall. "Beg pardon?"

"Don't you know a sneeze when you hear one?" The captain blew his nose.

She certainly didn't know *that* sneeze. It was a powerful amount of noise from such a small man, like a locomotive starting up. "Mis-sis-*sip*-pi, Mis-sis-*sip*-pi." She had not thought of it before, but that was exactly how an engine sounded, getting up steam.

"Well, God bless me," Captain Hetcher muttered, ignoring her surprised silence.

He scraped back the chair and strode to the fireplace, turned, and waggled a finger at Zoe. "And another thing. Get that bedspread from that tree. Flapped like a ghost all night."

"It won't be dry yet," Zoe objected.

"Damnable weather!"

Captain Hetcher slapped his hand against the man-

71

telpiece. Absently, he scraped his fingernails across the bricks, lingering on the seventh from the top. Zoe dug her own nails into her palm.

All of a sudden, he dropped his hand and pointed at the hearth. "Build a fire. This room is damp as a root cellar."

"Yes, sir!" said Zoe, so relieved she fairly shouted. She picked some sticks from the wood box and arranged them, tepee fashion, in the grate. They were moist to the touch, and the spark she struck hissed and went out. "Wood's a mite green," she apologized.

"Get some that will burn," the captain demanded. "No, never mind."

He crossed the room and pulled two of Papa's books from the shelf. Zoe clapped a hand over her mouth. One of the books in his hand was tied with twine. He tossed them into the fireplace, flattening the sticks, and then struck a sulphur match on the bricks. It flared, and he held it to the cover of the smaller volume. The binding began to singe, and the leaves within scorched.

"That should do it," Captain Hetcher said smugly.

A tongue of yellow flame darted up, licking the cover of the second book. The twine snapped and the old, brittle pages crackled. All Zoe could read was *Proverbs.*

"Oh, dear!" cried Zoe. A black cloud billowed out into the room. "Oh, dear me! I didn't open the damper!"

"What in tunket?" Choking, Captain Hetcher held his handkerchief to his face and fled from the parlor.

Zoe dashed the contents of the coffee cup onto the flames. The fire sputtered weakly for a few minutes and then died out. Smoke still floated in the room and Zoe opened the veranda windows wide, but the breeze was so slight it scarcely made the curtains sway. Eyes smarting, Zoe went back to the fireplace and rummaged in the ashes with the poker. Surprisingly, the small leather-bound book, *Common Sense*, by Thomas Paine, was only scorched, but a receipt had fallen from its pages and was too blackened to make out. The larger volume of charms and cures was ruined. Zoe blew the soot from the few remaining pages.

"I've another book here that might interest you, Miss Zoe Stewart Snyder."

Zoe turned around slowly. The young aide called Boone stood in the archway. And in his hand was her journal.

"Seems none of us rested well last night," he said, grinning. "This diary is too thick and my mattress was too thin."

He'd poked his nose in her journal! That was how he knew her name. Probably chuckled when he saw the Abracadabra.

"Is your eyesight poorly? That book is marked *Personal Property*," Zoe snapped.

Boone's smile faded. His face was serious as he handed her the journal. "I'd not pry into private thoughts."

Zoe clasped it tightly. Maybe all he'd seen was her name on the flyleaf, but you couldn't trust a Yankee. Thank heaven she'd not mentioned Papa's coming.

"Most obliged," she said stiffly and went out into the hall without meeting his eyes.

Threads of smoke, like the morning mist, drifted there,

73

too. Mama and Jim Henry stood just inside the open front door.

"I smelled that smoke and thought they'd fired the house!" cried Mama with a little flutter of relief.

Jim Henry held his nose. "I thought Zoe'd burned the biscuits!"

If there'd been enough left of *Proverbs* to whack him with, Zoe might have done just that. Instead she handed the ruined book to her brother. "Keep this for me," she said.

Mama looked sharply at the book and then at Zoe. "Breakfast," she said briefly, and she and Jim Henry went into the kitchen.

Boone gave Zoe a small smile and then wandered out onto the veranda. Zoe hesitated, still gripping her journal. She'd no means of writing in it. Everything was quiet overhead. She tiptoed up the stairs.

For one dreadful moment, Zoe thought someone was in her room. Boone's long underwear was draped over the back of her chair, the sleeves and legs dangling. She supposed Yankee drawers weren't much different from Papa's or Jim Henry's, and she'd washed those often enough. But in her own room, Boone's undersuit was almost as shameful as having the man here himself.

Zoe made a wide circle around the chair, stopping at the mirror to rub a spot of soot from her forehead. Her hair hung loose on her shoulders, and there were waves where the braids had been. It looked almost as nice as Letty's curls. Zoe twisted a lock around a finger, considering.

". . . And clean these boots!"

The captain's voice rose distinctly from the yard below. Zoe jumped guiltily. Here she was, preening, while Bluecoats paraded beneath her very window. She went quickly to the chest. A piece of paper lay upon it, and the bottle of ink was uncorked.

> *My dearest Emily,*
> *We have been in north Georgia some time now. . . .*

Zoe did not read any further. She had no more right to peep at Boone's letter to his sweetheart than he had to rifle through her journal. If he had. She lifted the ink bottle and then put it down again. If she took the pen and ink, he'd certainly guess she'd been snooping. The old goose quill pen would do well enough. And lots of folks made ink from mushrooms these days; she reckoned she could do the same from huckleberries. Lucky there were so many berries; she surely had plenty to say.

Monday
10

Zoe aimed to take her journal to Hodge's cabin straight-away. But it was past ten o'clock before all the pesky tasks were done and she could get out of the house. As she crossed the veranda, Boone waved at her.

"Miss Zoe!"

"Yes?" At least he said her name right, although in that horrid up-north way.

Boone had the basket of potatoes beside him and had peeled a dozen or more of them into a pot. "Ever seen the likes of this?" he asked.

Zoe kept a good distance between herself and the aide, concealing her journal behind her back. She couldn't make out what he held, but it was surely smaller than a potato. "What is it?"

"See for yourself. I found it a bit ago, buried at the bottom of the basket."

Zoe edged closer. Her tortoise-shell talisman lay in the palm of Boone's hand.

"Pretty little thing, isn't it? Never seen a trinket quite like this'n."

"That's mine!" Zoe blurted.

"Is it, now?" He grinned. "I thought to send it home to Emily."

"I lost it digging those taters. Give it to me!"

"Is that an order?" Boone sprang to his feet, holding the shell high, well beyond Zoe's reach. "Way I heard, it's finders keepers."

Zoe swallowed. "Please," she begged, "it's my good-luck charm."

Boone continued to dangle the charm over her head. "What does it do? Shall I rub it for three wishes?"

"No!" Zoe kept her eye on the talisman. "I mean, it might not work right for you."

"Just for you? Sounds like you're as superstitious as the cap."

"Captain Hetcher?"

"Yep." Boone lowered the shell slightly. "He's jumpy as a cottontail about any sort of hex. Throw a hat on the bed and he'll throw you out of the house."

Zoe stretched up her right hand. "A hat on the bed invites bad luck."

Boone lifted an eyebrow and raised the talisman once more. "Spooky!"

"I'm not . . . always." Zoe stepped back. She'd have to use caution. "I purely love black cats."

"And redskins?"

Her left hand tightened about her journal. "Why do you ask that?"

"That's what the captain really dreads. Indians, dead or alive. He's got some cause for that, though. Injuns are giving the army a heap of trouble out west."

"They got cause themselves," Zoe murmured. Hadn't that army forced the Cherokees off their own land and across the Mississippi?

Joshua Boone frowned. He seemed to have forgotten about the shell in his hand. Zoe was just about to make a grab for it when a high-pitched whoop burst from beyond the veranda. The aide snapped to attention, and Zoe jumped back, putting a decent number of floorboards between them.

Sergeant Morton thundered around the corner of the porch, but he was not alone. Jim Henry sat astride his shoulders.

"Jim Henry!" shrieked Zoe. That big devil had got hold of her brother!

"Whoa!" called Jim Henry, pulling on Morton's red hair. The sergeant skidded to a stop, panting.

"You put my brother down this instant—" Zoe began.

"Giddap!" Jim Henry kicked Morton sharply in the ribs.

Sergeant Morton responded with a silly sort of whinny and trotted across the drive.

Zoe made a start for the steps, but Boone grabbed her apron strings. "Let them be."

She wheeled about. "He's running off with my brother!"

" 'Pears more like your brother is running off with him," said Boone, pointing as mount and rider disappeared over the rise of the lane.

"That . . . cannibal!"

"Morton's got ten fingers and ten toes, same as you and me."

Zoe jerked violently. "I'll warrant that brute's got at least eleven."

"Go on and act foolish." Boone let loose of her apron. "Sergeant Morton's not about to harm Jim Henry. He's got two young'uns of his own. He misses them so much, he aches all over."

Zoe felt tears well. Her own brother, cavorting with the enemy! "Don't the rest of you Yankees depend on such friendly treatment."

"That so? Then I reckon I'll not return this just now." Joshua Boone thrust the tortoise shell into his pocket and turned back to the basket and his task of peeling.

"I reckoned you reckoned not to all along!" Zoe said hotly.

Boone did not reply. When he spoke again, his tone was carefully matter-of-fact. "I've got to save a red potato for the captain to carry in his waistcoat. He claims it cures the rheumatism."

He pared a potato, and shreds of peel, paper thin, fell to the floor. He flicked out the eyes with the tip of the knife, whistling through his teeth and working the blade as deftly as Mama handled a needle.

Zoe smiled timidly. She'd not back talk again. Catch

more flies with honey than vinegar anyhow. "I know that song." She tapped a foot as Boone sang. "That's 'Hey, Betty Martin.' "

"Hey, Betty Martin, tippy-toe, tippy-toe,
  Hey, Betty Martin, tippy-toe fine.
Hey, Betty Martin, tippy-toe, tippy-toe,
  Hey, Betty Martin, please be mine."

How peculiar! The same tune, the same words as folks sang around here! Zoe mouthed the words under her breath.

"Skip so fine, skip so fine. Skipping, skipping all the time!" finished Boone loudly, right along with her, as if the two of them were in a church choir.

She'd have no part of that! "You Bluecoats even steal our songs!"

"Seems you Rebels lay claim to everything," Boone answered. "I heard tell that's Mister Lincoln's favorite song."

"Lincoln!"

She'd like to teach this Joshua Boone a different tune. "Dixie"! Zoe shook the journal in her hand. "Well, this book is a personal possession. And that turtle shell you've got is mine, too!" She stamped down the veranda steps and called over her shoulder, "And those taters are ours as well, every last one of them!"

"Miss! Hold a minute!" Boone began, but Zoe did not turn. She crossed the gravel drive and went down the path to Hodge's cabin.

Monday, June 20, 1864
They are worse than can be believed. Trashing the
premises, even soiling the air . . .

Zoe took more than two full pages in her journal to
describe the Yankees, despite the fact that the huckleberry juice was so thin that it faded from purple to pink
as she wrote. She put down the pen and wriggled her
stiff fingers.

What would Emma Sanson do now? Could she out-
smart the enemy if they'd taken over her house, her
yard, were even sleeping in her own bed?

Zoe dipped the quill in the juice and stabbed it down
on the paper.

Most terrible of all is one by name of Joshua Boone.
First he had this journal. And now he's stole my
own talisman.

Monday
11

Zoe was late in returning to the house. It was past midday before she brought Captain Hetcher's dinner into the company parlor. He greeted her sullenly, as if he imagined she'd meant to smoke him out on purpose. Now another fire glowed in this grate, and only a few wisps of smoke curled up the chimney. Although the day was muggy, Captain Hetcher had drawn the cherrywood rocker close to the blaze. He was dressed in full uniform, save for his boots. Cleaned and polished, they dried on the hearth while the captain soaked his feet in a washtub of hot water.

"Feeling better, Captain?" Zoe asked, defensively polite. She balanced the tray on the footstool beside him.

He coughed in reply.

"My mother boiled up the bones for chicken broth, and the biscuits have just now come out of the oven." Trust Mama to fuss over anyone the least little bit ill, even an enemy!

Captain Hetcher gazed glumly at the soup. "Is this all?"

"Starve a cold . . ." Zoe began.

"You've got it twisted. It's *feed* a cold and *starve* a fever." He picked up the silver spoon and sipped the broth. "Needs salt."

The salt cellar with its tiny dipper sat beside the biscuits. The captain reached for it, and the tray tilted dangerously. As he steadied the soup bowl with one hand, he knocked over the salt with the other.

"Now look what you've gone and done!" he growled at Zoe. He scooped up a pinch of salt and threw it over his left shoulder. "Here's spit in the devil's eye!"

Zoe gawked at him.

"Ill luck to spill salt," the captain muttered, and dabbed with his napkin at the sweat that suddenly beaded on his bald head.

"I know that. I read—" began Zoe, but she was interrupted by the clock striking the half hour. She never did finish, for suddenly she had a splendid notion. There might be a different way to smoke out Captain Hetcher.

He drew the gold watch from his pocket. "That over-sized clock of yours is five minutes slow." Captain Hetcher snapped his watchcase shut with smug satisfaction.

"Now and then the clock runs fast or slow," said Zoe, "when something or someone has upset her."

"Seems that way," the captain agreed. He laid aside his spoon and drank his soup. "Upsets who?"

"Grandmama," Zoe replied. "That's her in the picture." She pointed at the portrait above the mantel. "The clock was hers. Her very favorite thing, poor soul." Zoe spoke the last words slowly and then sniffed.

Captain Hetcher looked uncomfortable. "She's passed on?"

"Grandmother has passed on, but not away, you might say. And such a way to die!"

"Don't bother with the details," Captain Hetcher mumbled through a mouthful of biscuit.

"Scalped," Zoe persisted. "Every lock of that shiny black hair was cut from her head. And then . . ." She drew her finger across her throat.

"Indians?" The captain's eyes widened with horror. "Here? In this house?"

"In this very room," said Zoe, shaking her head. "They murdered her and scalped her and stole most everything she owned. Of course they couldn't take her clock. It's too big."

Captain Hetcher stopped eating. He shivered, despite the heat from the fire.

"Did the soup disagree?" asked Zoe.

"No. No, burned my tongue a trifle, that's all."

Zoe ran the tip of her own tongue over the roof of her mouth, half expecting to discover bumps. Blisters broke out if you told a lie. Zoe turned away from the portrait of Grandmother Stewart. Grandmama was doubtless at that very moment eating dinner in Atlanta, and with far heartier appetite than the captain's.

"That's why she loves the clock," Zoe continued. "It's all Grandmother Stewart has left to return to in this mortal world. It's home for her unhappy spirit."

"She—comes back?"

"Well," Zoe hesitated. "We haven't exactly seen her. Usually we just notice the clock, speeding up or slowing down when she's troubled."

The captain looked skeptical. "Doesn't it bother you to have a haunt in the house?"

"Oh, no," answered Zoe. "Grandmama's family, after all." Her voice dropped to a whisper. "But she doesn't take to strangers. Sometimes we hear her footsteps pacing back and forth. And sometimes we hear a—shriek!" Zoe opened her mouth and screamed.

The captain jumped up, forgetting that his feet were soaking in the washtub. Water splashed in all directions.

"Like that," Zoe added.

Unghostly footsteps pounded down the stairs. Zoe stiffened as Sergeant Morton appeared in the archway.

"Everything all right in here, sir?" he asked.

Mama was right behind him. She pushed the sergeant aside as if he were no bigger than Jim Henry and ran straight to Zoe. "Are you hurt? That scream—"

85

"I'm sorry you got such a fright, Mama." Zoe patted her mother's arm. "It's nothing. Captain Hetcher just spilled a little salt."

Mama put her hands on her hips and glared, first at Zoe, then at the captain and the puddle on the carpet. "Well, Kingdom come!" she said finally.

Monday
12

Mama remained vexed all afternoon.

"I didn't mean to cause a stir," said Zoe to her mother by way of apology. She could not explain the circumstances in Papa's parlor without explaining her idea, and Mama would never approve of it, either.

"As if I've not worries enough, without such scenes as that. If you're going to make trouble, you'd better stay down at the cabin with Jim Henry."

"Yes'm."

Mama relented just a little. "It might be a good idea for you to keep an eye on him, anyway. I fret about the child down there alone, so close to the creek, with the water running high."

"I'll go this very minute." Zoe had another reason to be upset about her brother, but she knew better than to share it.

"Might as well clean him up while you're there," said Mama. She filled a pitcher with hot water from the reservoir in the stove and got a bar of strong lye soap.

When Zoe went down the hall, she saw Captain Hetcher in Papa's parlor, bent over the desk, rummaging in a leather dispatch case. Joshua Boone was no longer on the veranda, and only a couple of soldiers milled about. The captain had promised to keep them busy, and probably most were off following his orders. Or thieving. For whatever reason, Zoe was grateful to be able to walk through her own yard without curious stares.

The scattered clouds of early morning had given way to a solid ceiling of gray, and a light drizzle was falling. Zoe hurried. If Jim Henry was still out in this weather, he'd be soaked to the skin and catch cold, or worse.

She pushed open the cabin door and almost dropped the pitcher in surprise. Jim Henry sat quietly on the cot, dry as a dust ball, pretending to read the few remaining pages of *Proverbs, Maxims, and Curious Folk Beliefs.*

"Scamp! How'd you get down here?" Zoe demanded.

Jim Henry grinned. "Got me a ride."

"I know all about that ride. What are you thinking of, making up to a Yankee like that?"

Jim Henry bit his thumbnail. "Morton's nice."

"Nice! You yourself called him a devil."

"That was yesterday. Today he gave me this." Jim Henry put a small silver coin on the table. "A whole half dime for my bank!"

"Shame on you! Selling yourself to the enemy!" Zoe thumped the pitcher down on the table.

"But I wanted to see the little man tip his hat," Jim Henry wailed. Then he spied the pitcher. "Hey! Apple squeezings!"

Zoe shook her head. "Too early in the summer for cider. This here's scrubbing water."

"I'll wash in the creek like the soldiers."

"You'd wash, and that's a fact—straight downstream to the river." Zoe picked up a rag with one hand and took hold of her brother's arm with the other.

"Not my ears!"

"More dirt in them than in the potato patch." Zoe rubbed the washrag on his neck.

Jim Henry squirmed. "I've got something that's better than scrub water."

"What's that?"

"Look by the fireplace."

In the chimney corner Zoe saw a pail that surely had not been there when she left. She let go of her brother, knowing that was exactly what he'd hoped for, and walked over to it. The pail was full of newly pared potatoes, and a slab of fatback bacon, a bit green on the rind as if it had journeyed quite a distance, lay on top. Stuck to the handle was a note. The scrap of paper had obviously been torn from the bottom of a letter, but Zoe recognized the ink as her own.

I'm sure Captain Hetcher would wish to be a gentleman and share his your potatoes. J. Boone.

Zoe thrust her hand into the pail and felt about with her fingers, pushing aside the slippery peeled potatoes. No hard, slick shell hid among them. "Fiddle!"

"What's wrong?" asked Jim Henry.

"Nothing. Everything," said Zoe. She crumpled up the note and stuffed it in her pocket. Her hand brushed the letter opener. She'd forgotten all about it.

"It was nice of Josh to bring down the potatoes," objected Jim Henry. "Some Yankees aren't so terrible."

"That's something I want to talk to you about," Zoe answered over her shoulder. She poked kindling into the fireplace.

"Yankees?"

Zoe struck the flint, but the wood did not catch. "I think I know how to make my wishbone wish come true." What she wished she had right then was one of Captain Hetcher's sulphur-tipped matches.

"Chase away the Yankees?"

"If we can just get shed of that captain, the rest will follow."

The spark caught. Zoe pulled out the letter opener and sawed at the moldy rind on the bacon. When most of the green was off, she dropped the bacon along with the potatoes into the three-legged iron spider. Next she stirred in a little water from the pitcher, covered the skillet, and moved it over the blaze.

"One thing's for certain, you'll eat till you burst tonight," she promised Jim Henry.

Zoe washed the letter opener. It was a right handy tool, and a very special use for it had just occurred to her. When it was clean, she dipped the blade into the huckleberry juice that she had used for ink. She eyed it critically. The stain was more rose than red, but it would have to do.

Jim Henry watched her, curious. "What are you doing to Papa's letter opener?" he demanded.

Zoe waved the letter opener above her head to dry it. "I aim to use it for Captain Hetcher."

Her brother's eyes grew big as a bobcat's. "You're going to stab the captain!"

"I would not do such a thing even if I could." Zoe pulled out Joshua Boone's note, wrapped it about the opener, and returned both to her pocket.

"Is it a secret?" asked her brother.

"You mustn't breathe a word to a living soul."

"Not even Mama?"

"Especially not Mama. It wouldn't be right to mix her up in this."

"Cross my heart and soldier's honor," Jim Henry swore solemnly. "But what *is* it?"

Zoe was equally serious. "We're going to haunt Captain Hetcher. He's an awfully nervous man, and we're going to make him a powerful lot more nervy."

Jim Henry looked doubtful. "Mister Hodge told me not to rile the Yankees, and I'm not . . . now."

"You don't have to do anything different than usual. Just slam the door each time you go in and out of the house, so's the door to the clock will swing open."

"Is that all?"

"You get to be the ghost of the clock as well."

"A ghost! Can I moan?" Jim Henry flapped his arms and groaned.

"No! You must be still as a mouse." Zoe looked sternly at her brother. "Tomorrow, just at noon, I want you to hide in the clock and make it strike thirteen."

Jim Henry stared at the floor. "But I can't tell time with those Norman rumerals."

"That's Roman numerals." Zoe hugged him. "And you don't have to read the clock's face. Just count the strikes. After twelve, make the gong ring one more time."

"What are you going to do, Zo?"

"I'm not sure about tomorrow yet, but right now I'm going to wash your ears."

Tuesday
13

Zoe dawdled the next morning, letting Mama and Jim Henry go ahead up to the house. She hardly ever had a moment to herself, what with the three of them squeezed together in Hodge's cabin like new-hatched jaybirds in a nest. Zoe opened her journal and picked up the quill pen.

> Tuesday, June 21, 1864
> _Important!_

Zoe underlined the word twice.

> _Captain Hetcher holds some strange beliefs. He is especially feared of ghosts and Indians. So if there is a way to convince him our house is truly haunted, then we'll be rid of him and those other Bluecoats before . . ._

There! She almost went and wrote *before Papa comes!*

. . . it's too late.

She put down the pen. Perhaps *Proverbs* might have some sort of hex sign she'd missed. She blew the soot from the scorched pages. One sheet was just the index. Three were from the section on cures. Just reading them made her squeamish, the recipes were so terrible. The chapter on amulets and talismans was almost complete, but that only made her want her tortoise shell more than ever.

Another page from *Proverbs* had fallen to the floor. Zoe read aloud the verse on it. Why, this might have been written just for her! She copied it into her journal.

> *For every trouble under the sun*
> *There's a remedy, or there is none.*
> *If there be none, never mind it.*
> *If there be one, try to find it.*

"Try to find it!" Zoe repeated the words solemnly, as if she were taking an oath.

She slipped the pages of *Proverbs* into her journal. Then she patted her apron pocket, comforted by the feel of the letter opener within, and marched up the lane toward the house, toward Captain Hetcher.

It had stormed during the night, a real gully-washer. Zoe stopped to scrape her boots on the veranda steps, and sniffed. That was fresh coffee she smelled, real coffee. Whatever other orders Captain Hetcher had given his men yesterday, he'd not forgotten his own wants. She wrinkled her nose. A pity coffee did not taste as good as it smelled. The half-forgotten fragrance pulled her toward the kitchen.

It drew the captain from his room as well. He was buffed from head to boot, and both his smile and his mustache looked freshly waxed. Captain Hetcher was in such obvious high spirits that Zoe's own heart sank.

"Well! This is the way to start the day, eh?" He rubbed his hands together. "I'll take some of that coffee now, missy, if you please. In the library."

"Yes, sir, Captain."

The two passed in the hall and then both turned and looked back at the grandfather clock. The door to the case was open wide. Captain Hetcher lifted his eyebrow. He latched the door firmly and strode into Papa's parlor.

Zoe looked anxiously about the kitchen, but Jim Henry was nowhere to be seen. Mama had finished straining the coffee and had spread the grounds out to dry on a sheet of old newspaper.

"We'll boil these up again," she commented. "They'll be almost as good the second time around."

"A little bit of coffee, a whole lot of salt. Maybe we should thank the captain for his charity when he leaves," muttered Zoe.

Her mother leaned wearily against the stove. "Just pray that's quick. Here, child, might as well take him a cup."

There were purple shadows beneath Mama's eyes. Small wonder, having to sleep on Hodge's hard cot. If she'd slept at all. When Zoe and Jim Henry tucked in, Mama was still sitting in the chair, "thinking on things." Zoe knew what things. The Yankees. And what might happen if they were yet about when Papa returned.

Zoe sloshed some of the precious dark brew into the saucer as she stalked into Papa's parlor. She shoved it on the desk before the captain. Spirals of steam curled up from the cup, and bubbles clustered around the rim.

"Ah!" Zoe whispered hoarsely. "Bubbles in the cup! That means a visitor's arriving."

"That so?" The captain stirred the coffee, and the bubbles swirled about the spoon.

Zoe studied the coffee as if she were reading tea leaves and announced, "I do declare!"

"Declare what?" Wary, Captain Hetcher drew the cup closer and bent his pointy nose over the rim, as if he expected to find a doodlebug floundering within. His mustache began to uncurl in the steam.

Zoe crouched over the desk, her head close to the captain's. Her right arm circled the cup as she peered down, but her left hand slipped into her apron pocket. She withdrew the letter opener and silently slid it onto the desktop. Then she straightened and said, "It's what I don't see that matters. The bubbles have disappeared, every last one of them."

"Nothing unusual about that." The captain blew on the coffee to cool it.

"Not yet. But I suspect that means your visitor will be of a vanishing nature, Captain."

"Humbug!" Captain Hetcher took a sip. "The fact is

that I do expect a visitor today, one very much of this world."

Zoe plucked nervously at her apron. "Will there by anything else, sir? I'll lay a fire if you'd like."

"No!" he exploded. His glance fell upon the letter opener. "I thought I told you to clean this up."

"I did, Captain."

Captain Hetcher held up the opener. "It's still stained."

"So it is," agreed Zoe, "but it was the handle that was bloody yesterday. The blood's on the blade this time. Like always."

"Always?"

"Grandmama's last mortal act was to defend herself with this very letter opener. She drew blood from the Indian, but little good it did. Still, she tried." Zoe gestured toward the letter opener. "And keeps on trying to this very day, bless her restless soul."

Captain Hetcher dropped the opener in the desk drawer, slammed it shut, and turned the key in the lock. "Let's have an end to your ghost stories." He drank the coffee to the dregs and handed her the cup. "That will be all."

Zoe started down the hall to the kitchen. The door to the clock was ajar again. As she closed it, she was aware that Captain Hetcher was standing in the archway, staring.

Captain Hetcher left the house shortly thereafter, taking Sergeant Morton with him. As soon as they had departed, Joshua Boone poked his head in the door.

"Are you free to go walking?" he asked Zoe.

"No!" she answered sharply, adding "The ground's much too muddy underfoot."

"I'd like a word with you."

"We've got nothing in common to talk about," Zoe retorted.

Boone looked disappointed. She supposed she might have thanked him for the potatoes, but he had already gone down the steps.

Zoe took the feather duster into the company parlor and swished it absently around the room, raising more dust than she removed. She glanced apologetically at the portrait of Grandmother Stewart. "I'm sorry to misuse you. But being as I'm your namesake, perhaps you'll understand."

It seemed to Zoe that Grandmama's eyes narrowed and inspected both her and the parlor with disapproval. Defiantly, she flicked the feather duster over that lady's nose. Grandmother would have an attack of the vapors if she could actually see the muddy footprints the Yankees had left on the carpet. Despite a soap-and-water scrubbing, ugly dark shadows remained. Zoe studied the rug. Grandmama had given it to Mama as a wedding present.

"Why, hunky-dory!" she exclaimed.

That was a new Jim Henry word, but it fit her situation just like—like an old shoe? Zoe grinned. The way to shake up Captain Hetcher—to send him trotting—lay right there at her feet.

The first thing Zoe saw when she returned to the cabin was the page from *Proverbs*, the one with the verse. It lay in the middle of the floor. Zoe recalled tucking it into her journal. And where *was* her journal? Not on the table where she'd left it. Zoe picked up the paper. Nothing else was out of order in the cabin that she could see. The coals were banked in the fireplace. The quilt was tidily pulled up on Mama's cot. The bearskin rug was slightly askew, the fur still ruffled from Jim Henry's flopping about. Zoe checked her own pallet. Beneath the pillow was her book, pressed open to the page she had written earlier. She never would have done that!

Zoe looked uneasily over her shoulder. No way to lock the cabin when no one was here. The drawstring pulled from the inside. So anyone at all might have walked right in.

Papa!

He had been the morning visitor. He'd come home and he'd seen those Yankees spread everywhere, so he'd hustled down to the cabin. Then he'd seen her journal—his ledger—and he'd read it and slipped it under her pillow as a sign. But why hadn't he left a sign for Mama, too?

Zoe had another, less happy, notion.

Joshua Boone!

He had gone walking, sure enough, and walked directly to their cabin. Then he'd snooped in her journal again. Zoe ran her finger under the words she'd written.

She'd never said how she would get rid of Captain Hetcher, because she'd not known the answer yet. As for mention of Indians and superstitions, why, Joshua Boone himself had told her that. And probably lots of folks knew that verse, even some up north. Little good his spying had done him!

She sat down at the table and dipped the pen into the huckleberry juice. Beneath the verse she printed in bright-pink letters,

I FOUND THE REMEDY!

If Papa saw that, he'd know that she knew he'd been here. And if Joshua Boone saw it, he'd not know a thing more than he knew already.

Tuesday
14

"Late again! It's past noon," Captain Hetcher grumbled when Zoe brought his tray into the company parlor.

"How were we to know you would be back for dinner?" asked Zoe, surprised by her own boldness. "Anyway, the clock's not yet struck."

"That timepiece is plagued!" retorted the captain. "It's ticking slower than a funeral march." He took the cover off the dish she set before him. "Mush!"

"Mush is good for you if you're feeling poorly."

"Pig food!" The captain stabbed at the yellow slices of fried mush. "Inform your mother I expect a more imaginative supper."

If Mama would let her fix Captain Hetcher's vittles, she'd put imagination and a whole lot more into them! Zoe had more sense than to speak her thoughts. The smile she gave the captain was as sweet as sorghum, but the only sound was the ticking of the clock. It whirred softly and then struck.

". . . Ten . . . eleven . . . twelve," Zoe counted. Still smiling, she addressed the captain. "There doesn't seem to be anything ailing the clock."

"My watch says ten past the hour," Captain Hetcher began, but he was interrupted. A single hollow note from the clock floated down the hall like an afterthought.

"Thirteen!" exclaimed Zoe.

Captain Hetcher pushed aside his plate and flung his napkin to the floor. "I'll get to the bottom of this!"

"Let me see to it," Zoe volunteered hastily. "Grandmama hates to have strangers fussing."

The captain had already stamped out under the arch and into the hall. He jerked open the door of the clock. Zoe gasped. Poor Jim Henry!

Together, they looked inside the clock. The captain turned as pale as a peeled potato. Except for the weights and the brass pendulum, swinging steadily back and forth, the case was empty. Zoe closed her eyes and slumped against the wall. Never, never again would she underestimate her brother.

Captain Hetcher cleaned his plate in silence. Then he snapped, "I'm expecting someone. I'll be in the library."

Zoe took the tray back to the kitchen. Mama sat at the table, holding her head in her hands.

"I've not seen hide nor hair of Jim Henry all morning. He's missed his dinner," she said unhappily.

"Jim Henry's able to take care of himself," Zoe reassured her. "Why don't you rest for a bit, Mama?"

"I feel a headache coming." Mama rubbed her forehead. "Jim Henry might be at the cabin. Maybe I will lie down."

"Do that," urged Zoe. "I can manage absolutely everything here at the house."

What splendid luck! Captain Hetcher busy and Mama resting. But she hadn't a moment to spare, for no telling when Morton or some other nosy body might come bursting in.

The door to Mama's room was closed, and Zoe opened it cautiously. A whiff of stale cigar smoke and boot polish greeted her. She tiptoed to the trunk in the corner and lifted the lid.

Beneath the layers of pillowslips, bed sheets, and lace doilies was Mama's wedding dress, wrapped in linen. Zoe pushed the gown aside. At the very bottom of the trunk was a pair of white satin slippers. She picked them up. From toe to heel they measured scarcely eight inches, and were slender as a ruler. Her own feet had spread from going barefoot, just as Mama had warned. But even her mother could not wear such bitty shoes now. They were keepsakes from those Atlanta days when Miss Mary Alice had only to step from couch to carriage.

They were the perfect size for a ghost.

As Zoe crept back down the hall, she heard a commotion on the front veranda. She darted into the company parlor and ducked behind the lace curtain.

"You there! HALT!" That bellow had to belong to Sergeant Morton. "Stand as you are!"

That overstuffed Bluebelly, who's he stopped? He'd not dispute one of his own men, and who else . . .

"Oh, glory!" The words strangled in Zoe's throat. "Papa!" He *had* been at the cabin this morning, and now Morton had caught him!

"Release me this minute, sir!"

Zoe dropped the shoes. It couldn't be! She pulled aside a corner of the curtain and peered out. Morton held Letitia Jane McFee firmly by the shoulders.

"First explain, if you will, miss, what you were doing beneath that window." Morton nodded toward Papa's parlor, now Captain Hetcher's library.

"Not doing anything at all," Letty protested, wriggling beneath Morton's hand like a puppet on a string, " 'cepting to see if my school friend Zoe Snyder was to home."

School friend! Zoe nearly choked.

"It would seem more friendly to pay a call by knocking at the door," the sergeant accused.

Morton was right about that. There was something mighty peculiar about Letty's sneaking around. Something peculiar about her coming around at all. Zoe inched the curtain open. She didn't see any buggy. How had Letty slipped away from her mama?

After a long minute's silence, Letty replied, "I didn't want to raise any fuss. Because her mother needs peace and quiet," she added.

"This is no longer the Snyder home," Morton snapped. "It is Union army quarters."

"Dear me!" Letty gave a shrill giggle. "I had not heard the news."

"Humph!" Zoe sputtered. No telegraph ever spread gossip faster than Mrs. Postmaster McFee. And Letty could hardly miss seeing all those horses and men and mules.

"This property is quarantined," Morton added.

"Quarantined!" exclaimed Letty. "I do hope the sickness isn't catching."

"Not that kind of quarantine." Morton cleared his throat. "I mean no trespassing. None to come in and none to go off the premises." His voice was no longer so gruff. "I can't credit how you slipped past the sentries."

Zoe wondered how, and why besides. Letty was up to something sly. Maybe she was trading Southern secrets for sugar!

Letty sounded sweet enough now. "Why, I left my carriage down by the road and came up through the fields," she said. "So much quicker, you know, and I was on an errand for my mama and hadn't but a moment to spare. It seemed a pity to be so close and not drop by. Inconsiderate not to inquire as to the well-being of Zoe's mother—"

"Next time consider again before you go sashaying through Union lines." Morton loosened his grip on her shoulders. "I'll not report you if you leave as quick as you came."

"My pleasure, sir." Letty was already tapping down the steps.

Sergeant Morton clomped heavily after her. "Boone!" he shouted. "See that this young lady goes direct to her carriage."

Zoe and Morton could agree about that! The quicker Letitia McFee left, the better. Zoe saw Joshua Boone come around the corner of the veranda at a near gallop and take Letty's elbow. He must be pleased as punch to have someone willing to go walking. Zoe couldn't make out what they said, but she saw Letty's bonnet bouncing up and down as she tossed her head, and she heard Boone laugh. A turncoat and a Bluecoat!

Zoe dropped the curtain and picked up the shoes. Whatever else Letty might be scheming, she'd almost spoiled Zoe's own plan. She'd really have to hurry now. Morton was still out in the yard, and it would take but twenty minutes for Joshua Boone to get down to the road and back.

The remains of yesterday's fire were still in the grate. Zoe thrust her hands into the slippers and deliberately rubbed the soles in the ashes. She pressed first the right and then the left onto the blue carpet. Beside the larger tracks that the men had made, the small shoes left delicate, silvery impressions. She dusted them with ashes again and made a pattern of ghostly gray footsteps down the center of the room.

"My, my! Some unhappy spirit's been pacing through this parlor," Zoe said softly.

She eyed her work with satisfaction. Of course, a really close inspection would show that the prints were nothing more than fireplace soot. She had to count on Captain Hetcher being so startled he'd not think to check them right away. Even if he were suspicious, he would never call Morton or anyone else. He'd not want to appear the fool before other Damnyankees. If he decided to investigate later, she would have rubbed the footprints out. A truly disappearing visitor. That should convince the captain to quit a haunted house. If it didn't, nothing would.

Zoe felt a twinge of guilt, but it was for the smudged shoes in her hand. They'd never come clean. Mama would have to throw them away. Once more, Zoe rubbed the slippers in the ashes. She tiptoed into the hall and knelt on the floorboards. The last tiny tracks must lead from the clock. One footprint. Two. A third.

"Mis-sis-*sip*-pi!"

There was no mistaking that sneeze. A shadow fell across the floor, and where the fourth print should rightly have gone were two black-stockinged real feet.

"May I ask," said the harsh voice above her head, "exactly what you are up to?"

"I—I thought—" Zoe began. She pressed her cheek against the floor. Captain Hetcher had proved no fool. She was.

"You've done quite enough thinking already," barked Captain Hetcher. "It is evident that you are behind the mumbo jumbo in this household."

107

Zoe did not reply. She was certain she'd melt away. When Mama came to find her, there'd only be a spot on the floorboards.

"Granny ghosts! Injuns!" The captain sneezed again and blew his nose. There was silence. Zoe waited and then looked up. Captain Hetcher was putting away his handkerchief in one pocket and taking out a cigar from the other. He leaned deliberately against the clock for a moment before he pulled out a sulphur match. He rasped the tip across the Cherokee rose and a blue flame flared.

"I know how I will even our score, missy," he said.

The flame flickered to yellow. Captain Hetcher lit the cigar and blew out the match. Then his stockinged feet padded into Papa's parlor as soundlessly as they had come.

It took enormous effort for Zoe to stand up. With the satin slippers still dangling from her hands, she ran out the door—and straight into Joshua Boone.

"Zoe!" he exclaimed, jumping aside.

Zoe shook her head. She could not trust herself to speak. She fled around the corner of the veranda and threw the ruined shoes under the honeysuckle bush. For a moment, she considered crawling beneath it herself. Bee stings couldn't make her hurt any worse. But hiding wouldn't do any good. She had to fix supper for the captain and then serve it, look right into those beady eyes, and watch a smirk twitch beneath his mustache.

What actually happened dumbfounded Zoe even more. Captain Hetcher ignored her. He acted as if she were invisible, and silence hung thick as a thundercloud in the parlor. When Zoe finally escaped to the cabin at sundown, her stomach was close to splitting with tears she couldn't cry. Maybe her face had swollen up with mortification, too, like the mumps, for Jim Henry hopped about, peskier than a flea, staring at her. He dared not question Zoe in front of Mama, and Mama herself was too anxious to notice anyone else's upset.

"I heard one of the Yankees say today that they lost twelve thousand men in the fighting at Cold Harbor." Mama wrinkled her apron between her fingers. "I don't like to dwell on how many of our own we won't see again."

Zoe knew what her mother left unsaid. She could not mention Papa with Jim Henry listening. Even when it was just the three of them together, away from the Yankees, they were separated by secrets.

"Nothing we can do about anything," Mama went on. "My own home is a jail with a score of soldiers as my jailors. I cannot step foot beyond my own fence posts."

That added to Zoe's miseries. In her personal war on Captain Hetcher, she'd nigh on forgotten the real war. Now her mischief would surely bring more troubles. All Zoe was able to say was "I'm right tired tonight, Mama."

She could be honest about that. She was more bone-and-brain weary now than when she'd faced up to the bear. Zoe lay down on her pallet, back to the fire, quilt over her head. She slept without dreaming until an ember popped and sputtered in the fireplace. She jerked, only half awake.

The glow from the coals threw huge, strange shadows on the rough log walls. Zoe propped herself up on an elbow. Now she could make out the familiar sharp shapes of the table and chair and the round lump on the floor that was her brother asleep on the bearskin. She let out her breath slowly. Zoe, Mama, and Jim Henry were safe in Mister Hodge's cabin.

But tomorrow was coming. Suddenly she was wide awake and sure of what was going to happen. She could see it plain as anything, like a play being acted out in a firelight. Captain Hetcher would strike another match against the clock. Then he'd give the order. "Burn this confounded timepiece!"

That's how the captain would even the score.

Wednesday
15

In the morning, Zoe's eyes were sandy and scratchy, as if she'd cried a bucketful. Mama put a cool hand on her forehead.

"You're feverish, child. You've been out too much in this wet without your bonnet, and it's done you no good to sleep on that damp floor."

"It's nothing," Zoe answered, diving down beneath the bedclothes.

"Stay where you are," Mama said firmly. "I'll tend to things alone today." She tucked the quilt about Zoe's shoulders.

Zoe did not protest. She really did feel poorly. She closed her eyes again and dozed. When she awakened, the cabin was stuffy, even with the door ajar. Zoe touched her cheek. She was hot, just as Mama said. If she caught the pneumonia and died, everyone would forgive her. They'd say how helpful she'd been and . . .

Zoe threw back the covers abruptly. She wasn't sick. She had to stop making things up. That's how she'd gotten tangled up in this trouble in the first place. She'd got the idea of scalping Grandmama from Letty McFee, and it had been that Joshua Boone who had put her onto the captain's superstitions. Fiddling about with the letter opener and the slippers had been all her own notion. Maybe hopping about in one shoe had really started it all.

Now Captain Hetcher was going to burn the clock. He might be so provoked at her, he'd fire the whole house! When Papa came home, there'd be nothing standing but the chimney. Unless . . .

Zoe got up. The captain was not vexed with Mama. He'd not be eating were it not for her. And he scarcely noticed Jim Henry. His grudge was against Zoe personally. If she weren't here to spite, perhaps Captain Hetcher would not be so vengeful.

Zoe splashed cold water on her face. Mister Hodge had left, hadn't he? Gone off, maybe all the way to the Oklahoma territory to be with his own people. She could go somewhere, too. She did not need to stay here and wait for the worst. Mama was truly confined, with the baby coming, but Zoe wasn't. If Letitia Jane McFee could slip past a sentry, so could she. She'd run away.

Deciding on a thing was almost as good as doing it. Zoe felt better. She was going to vanish, like a genuine ghost! She could picture the baffled look on Captain

Hetcher's face. No way he could settle a score with a spook!

She gathered her few clothes, stuffed them into an empty cornmeal sack, and put the bundle in the chimney corner. She'd best wait until dark to leave, and even then she dared not risk bidding good-bye to Mama and Jim Henry. And she'd miss greeting Papa, not see him at all. Maybe she'd never see any of them again, not in this mortal world. Zoe got a lump, big as a goose egg, in her throat.

She could leave a message in her journal so they'd not doubt why she'd gone, would not think she did not love them. "It's the written word that is important," Papa had said. "Why, without it, we'd know little about Caesar, or how Hannibal crossed the Alps, or about our own General Washington, when you come right down to it. . . ."

Zoe sighed. She guessed she'd come right down to it, as far down as she hoped she'd ever go. She picked up the quill.

> *Wednesday, June 22, 1864*
> *To those who read these words:*
> *Please do not think ill of me. If anything I have said or done causes hardship, I am truly sorry. My intent was to help my family, but it will be better for all if I go. . . .*

Leaves rustled and a branch cracked sharply. The mysterious visitor! He'd come sneaking back. Next thing he'd push right in and trap her like a rabbit. Zoe dropped the pen and squeezed behind the open door. If she just had a piece of kindling wood . . . But she'd never call up the nerve to whack a head anyhow. She shut her eyes and whispered, "Go away! Go away!"

"Mum's the word, now."

That was Morton's voice! Zoe opened one eye, squinted through the crack, and saw the sergeant swing Jim Henry down from his shoulder. Then Morton put a finger to his lips and winked. Those two were in cahoots about something!

"Git in here, Jim Henry!" Zoe shouted.

As soon as her brother was safe inside, she slammed the door and pulled the drawstring. Jim Henry sat cross-legged on the bearskin with Zoe glaring down at him.

"What's this all about?" she demanded.

"Nothing," Jim Henry answered defiantly, and then added, "Something. Mama said not to bother you, but I need to ask you something."

Zoe bit her lip. She couldn't put him off any longer. She'd have to tell him how she'd snared herself in her own trap. He deserved to know. "What is it?"

"Are all spies bad?"

Zoe gazed at him. There was never any telling what went through her brother's head. She chose her words carefully, one by one, like stepping stones. "I reckon it all depends," she answered, "on why you spy. If it's for a lark, or selfish reasons, then it's wrong. But if you're trying to help others, maybe even save some lives, then it's just a job that needs doing."

114

Jim Henry looked relieved. "I think I'm a spy. I was in the clock yesterday—"

"You did your part splendidly." Zoe managed to smile at him. "However did you disappear like that?"

"I was quiet as a mouse," said Jim Henry. "And quick as one, too. When I heard the captain coming, I scatted out the back door and behind the rain barrel." He stopped, pleased, and Zoe nodded. "Later on I sneaked back inside the clock and listened."

"What did you hear?" asked Zoe. Jim Henry would sure enough say he'd overheard that shameful scene between Captain Hetcher and herself.

"I know I'm not to eavesdrop on you and Mama," Jim Henry protested, "but I couldn't help hearing what that man and the captain said because they hollered at each other."

"What man?"

"I couldn't see his face, not inside the clock. But his voice didn't sound like one of *our* Yankees."

Captain Hetcher's visitor! "Go on."

" 'My scouts report General Johnston is firmly in the fence.' That's what he said, and then Captain Itch cussed and got het up as a hornet."

"In the fence?" Zoe tried to picture General Joe Johnston, bald head glistening, perched upon a rail fence.

"I think."

"That doesn't make sense at— entrenched!"

"I reckon maybe that's what I heard." Jim Henry nodded. "Anyway, this other man answered that General

Sherman don't care about nothing, he's so tired of marching and chasing Little Joe Johnston." Jim Henry frowned, as if puckering up his forehead might help him remember. "He said Sherman was going to attack the Rebs on Kennesaw Mountain, come hell or high water!"

"Jim Henry!"

"I didn't say that. The man did."

"But Kennesaw Mountain! Did he say when?"

"The man left. And I was hungry, so I got out of the clock."

Zoe regarded Jim Henry gravely. "No real soldier ever did better."

Jim Henry jumped up and clicked his heels. "Have you got more orders for me, Zo?"

"No." Zoe walked over to the table and rested a hand on her journal. "Anything else to be done I've got to keep to myself."

Jim Henry sniffed. "Then I'm not going to tell you what Morton calls me, neither." He giggled. "Mosquito!"

Zoe shook her head. Of course that sergeant would warn Jim Henry to keep mum. Didn't want her to know how friendly the two of them had got. How could she blame her brother for wanting company? The only person in all of Georgia to blame today was herself. And General Sherman.

Wednesday
16

"Let me in this minute!"

Zoe loosened the drawstring and swung open the door. Mama stepped over the threshold.

"There you are!" she said, but she walked right past Zoe. For once Mama was really riled with Jim Henry. She was about to shake the daylights out of him, but she couldn't, what with a bucket in one hand and the teapot in the other.

"I've been working," said Jim Henry. He waved the piece of paper that Zoe had ripped out for him from her journal. Letters, scribbled in charcoal, covered the page from top to bottom. "Real writing! ABC's!"

Zoe had been too caught up in her own thoughts to pay heed to her brother. Now she gaped. Jim Henry hadn't written the alphabet. That was the Abracadabra charm! It was Jim Henry who'd been peeking in her journal. No mistake about that!

"You worry me out of my wits, always disappearing," Mama scolded. "I told you not to go bothering your sister."

"I'm feeling all right, Mama," Zoe admitted.

Mama walked to the table and put down the bucket and the teapot. "Well, I'm not." Her hand trembled as she poured a cup of tea. "Drink this."

Zoe drank it dutifully. Sassafras. She should have known.

"Such a day! I'm completely tuckered." Mama sighed. "Captain Hetcher's been simmering like he's going to boil over. He nattered at me and harrassed that Joshua Boone near to death." She sat down heavily on Hodge's bed and drew off her shoes. "Maybe it's just as well Jim Henry kept out from underfoot. I'm not going back up to the house myself, not with the state that Hetcher's in. He can just wash up his own supper dishes."

"Supper!" Jim Henry eyed the bucket. "What's in there?"

"Greens," said Mama. "All that greedy man left."

Jim Henry's lip stuck out so far that Zoe could have hung her apron on it. But he didn't fuss. He cleaned his plate right down to the Chinese pattern and fell to sleep on the bear rug before sunset. Zoe looked down at him. He'd often gone to bed hungry these past months. No wonder he was so puny. When she got home again, she'd fill him up so full he'd never fit in the clock again.

As if reading her mind, Mama said, "He'll be grown up like you before we know it."

Like you! One thing about Mama, she was believable. If she said it, it was so. "Do you think someone can grow up all of a sudden?"

"Everyone grows in fits and starts, some quicker than others," her mother replied. "You can't take the outside measure just in inches. A lot of growing up takes place inside." Mama closed her eyes and lay back on the cot. "But that shows, too."

Zoe looked anxiously at her mother. "Are you . . . all right?"

"For the time being," Mama answered. She took a deep breath. "And resting, while I can."

Zoe walked slowly to the bed. What she wanted to do right now was bury her face on Mama's shoulder and spill out how foolish she'd been. She'd feel so much better for the telling, but hearing about Captain Hetcher's spite would make Mama feel worse. "Mama," said Zoe, "I got a name for the baby, if she's a girl . . . Emma."

"Emma." Mama's eyelids fluttered. "It's a proud name, though not so fine as Zoe."

"My name's just a hand-me-down from Grandmama."

"Zoe is Greek," said Mama. "For God's gift, if I recollect."

For pity's sake! Here she'd carried that name for nigh on thirteen years and nobody'd bothered to explain. God's gift! Had she but known, she'd have liked it better all along.

Zoe squeezed her mother's hand. Perhaps Mama had done some changing, too. Lately she'd begun talking to Zoe, not at her. "Mama," Zoe began, but she did not finish. Her mother was asleep.

Zoe wished she knew what time it was. She couldn't make herself sit still, and she checked over her bundle. Not much in it, but that would make it easier to tote. Mister Hodge had not taken much when he left, either. She propped her notebook on the table, with a corncob holding the page open with her message. She couldn't rightly call it a journal anymore, not with folks reading it like a newspaper.

Maybe she should say something more. Zoe nibbled on the end of the quill. If the Yankees were going off in just a few days, if what Jim Henry had overheard was right, then perhaps she could stay put. . . . No, she couldn't, either. She had to pass the word about General Sherman and Kennesaw Mountain. Billy Joe Judson would know what to do. And then she had to go on. Even if the Yankees were leaving, it only took a few seconds to strike a match. She'd start off north, toward Hiawassee, and see if someone would give her board in swap for chores. Zoe put down the pen. There wasn't anything meaningful that she was able to say.

She stood at the cabin door. For the longest time, the sun seemed stuck between the hills. Then they, too, fell into shadow, and she watched the first stars flicker on in the sky. The clouds had lifted and it was a fine evening, mild and clear. The chirps of tree frogs mingled with the rise and fall of men's voices from the fields beyond, and the moon climbed above the treetops. It hung suspended, huge and almost perfectly full, silver as the half dime Morton had given Jim Henry.

It did not matter what hour the clock showed. It was time to go.

Wednesday
~ 17 ~

Despite the warmness of the night, Zoe pulled the cloak close about her. The drab cloth would help her blend into the shadows. Moonlight outlined the path to the creek, and she could make out the wooden bridge ahead. The water had gone down some, and the planks were no longer awash. Zoe licked her lips. They were dry and left a salty tang on her tongue.

"Halt!"

A figure stepped out from behind the well house, and moonlight glinted on the barrel of a rifle.

Zoe froze. "Don't shoot!"

"Zoe?" Joshua Boone moved out of the weeds and onto the path. "Whatever brings you here?"

Although he had lowered the gun, in full uniform Boone looked menacing. His silhouette against the moon loomed as large as Morton's. Zoe hunched her shoulders, squeezing an elbow tight against her bundle. "I've—an errand," she stammered.

"I hardly thought you'd come to keep me company," Boone answered, "although standing sentry's mighty lonely."

"I've got to go cross creek and over to the Judsons'."

"Peculiar hour to go calling."

This Bluecoat was bound to spoil everything! "That's not your concern." Zoe lifted her chin. "Please stand aside, Mister Boone."

"Josh," he answered. "And it *is* my concern. Cap's orders are that none shall leave this property."

"This is a matter of . . . necessity."

"Your ma?"

She hadn't been thinking about that at all. But if he chose to believe her mission was about the baby, then let him. "Missus Judson is going to midwife," she said. That was no lie.

"My watch is creek patrol." Joshua Boone looked down at the buttons on his coat, as if all of a sudden he'd taken a notion to count them. At last he said, "Maybe I could come with you, as a guard. If I kept an eye on you—"

"I'm not afraid to go by myself."

He shook his head. "A scout spotted someone in the woods a while ago."

Papa! "Who?"

"Don't know who, don't know why." He took her elbow. "But I'll make certain you don't run into any trouble."

Zoe almost dropped her bundle! "No! I don't want you anywhere near!"

Joshua Boone looked as if she'd slapped him.

"It's not you personal I mean. It was mighty nice of you to offer." Zoe shook her head. "Makes me wonder why you wanted to take up fighting in the first place."

"Why did your daddy go off to war?"

"That's different!" Zoe jerked back like she'd been burned. "Papa went to save our home. And to keep strangers from telling us what we could and couldn't do."

"That's why I'm here then. To tell you what you can't do. To say one man cannot own another."

"We're not slave owners, if that's what you're getting to," Zoe retorted hotly. "But that fact never stopped you Yankees from marching all over us!"

"Ssssh," warned Boone, and Zoe was suddenly aware she'd been shouting. "I've a duty here," he added.

"I suppose it's your duty to bully women and children."

"I'd sooner be home in my own bed this night instead of wondering if some bushwhacker's going to put a bullet in my back. But I aim to keep my vow—and to keep the Union from splitting right down the middle."

"That split's come already." Zoe's voice was softer now. "When Papa left, he was part of a whole parade of loyal Georgians."

Zoe could still see the pageant that had been played out on the patch of grass before the courthouse. They'd hoisted the Stars and Bars to the top of the pole, and the flag had snapped in the breeze, its colors as bright as fresh paint. A fife shrilled and a boy beat the drum, keeping the time as man after man joined the ranks. Zoe'd been so proud of her tall father that she'd cheered until her throat was sore.

"Didn't seem like war," she said aloud. "More like a fair, or a barn raising."

"When I signed up, it was like the Fourth of July." Joshua Boone leaned against a tree. "There were sky-rockets and speeches and singing. And a whole mountain of food. The womenfolk filled us so full of cakes and pies, it was a wonder anyone could march at all."

Womenfolk. Zoe hadn't thought about Yankees having mothers. Or wives. Children, even.

"Most of us didn't consider what battle would mean." Joshua Boone turned to Zoe. "I'll wager that much is true for both sides."

Zoe nodded. There was a lot she hadn't stopped to consider. "Maybe underneath that ugly blue uniform you're not all that different from me," she said.

"Begging your pardon, but I'd allow I am." Joshua Boone coughed.

Zoe could feel her cheeks flush. Of course he was a he and she was a she. He mistook her meaning on purpose. "What I meant was you couldn't tell a Green Mountain man from one of our own Blue Ridge," she said, adding, "unless he was silly enough to speak out."

There was a sudden splash in the brook. Both of them jumped and then looked sheepishly at each other.

"Fish," said Zoe.

"Heard the catfish were biting," he answered.

They stared at the silver glints of moonlight in the dark water. Zoe reckoned that Joshua Boone's mind was fixed on the same things as her own—not on the fishing but on the fighting both knew was sure to come. "Are you scared of being killed?" she asked abruptly.

"No more'n anyone else." His low voice was almost drowned out by the gurgle of the creek. "Not a whole lot less, either."

Zoe was silent.

Joshua Boone cleared his throat. "I've been aiming to talk with you."

"I've been busy."

"And give you this." He reached into his pocket and pulled out the tortoise-shell talisman. He'd strung a thong through the hole and buffed the shell until it shone nearly as brightly as the brass buttons on his coat.

Zoe put out her hand. "I supposed you had sent it to your sweetheart. Emily."

Boone laughed and once again dangled the talisman over her head. "Emily's no sweetheart. Not most of the time, anyway." He lowered the shell, letting it drop about her neck like a locket. "You put me in mind of her. Emily's my little sister."

Little sister! Why, even Mama allowed how grown-up she was getting. Still, she'd got back the shell, and that's what mattered. The moon was full, and its magic should be the strongest.

"I may be in need of this luck," she said.

Joshua Boone frowned. "Counting on a charm is just

wishful thinking. How things go is up to you. A person makes his own luck."

He surely sounded brotherly, spilling over with advice. She'd not lose the shell again, whatever he said. Zoe tugged on it. The thong was knotted tight. She supposed it was one of Boone's own shoelaces.

"I'd have returned it before, but you never would give me the time of day."

Time of day! If she stood here much longer, it would be sun-up before she knew it. "I've got to hurry." All of a sudden Zoe felt awkward. "Take care, Mister Boone," she murmured.

"Take care of yourself, Miss Zoe Stewart Snyder." Then he doffed his cap as if she were a real lady, sixteen at least.

Zoe hurried across the bridge, but she hesitated on the other side. Although Boone had disappeared behind the well house, she could hear him whistling softly, "Hey, Betty Martin"!

By day, Zoe had often sneaked away to these woods, taking a book to read beneath the cool green canopy of leaves. Now the tangled branches wove a tunnel of darkness, and only an occasional moonbeam found its way through to the undergrowth below. But what she'd told Joshua Boone was true. She was not afraid. If Papa was about, he would take care of everything.

Each time some bush rustled unexpectedly, or a twig snapped, Zoe hesitated and whispered, "Papa?" There was no answer.

Once she could have sworn she saw a tall shadow slip behind a tree. "Wait!" she'd dared to shout, and raced up the trail.

No one hid behind the trunk, but she kept on running from tree to tree until a stitch in her side made her stop. She gulped back the bitter syrup that rose up in her mouth. Her mother would say that came from running, too, but Zoe knew better. What she tasted now was disappointment. Papa was not here. He would never lead her on such a chase, like a fox running off from a hound.

It was a waste of time to follow a phantom. That Yankee scout was doubtless drunk. If he'd seen a white-tailed deer, he would have reported an elephant. She wasn't going to let her imagination gallop off with her again.

Zoe picked her way back to the path and trudged on to the Judsons'.

Wednesday
18

Billy Joe Judson answered her knock. He opened the door a crack, bracing his shoulder against it. When the light from his candle fell on Zoe's face, he swung it wide open.

"Hello there, Zo." Billy Joe did not seem the least startled to see her standing on his stoop. "Is it my mother you want?"

"It's you," Zoe said, relieved it was Billy himself to greet her. "I hope you can help with something."

Billy Joe looked mildly surprised but nodded, and Zoe stepped through the door and into the front room. It served as nursery as well, for the newest Judson slept in a cradle by the fireplace. Zoe kept her voice low as she repeated what Jim Henry had heard.

"So that's what stands to happen," said Billy Joe when

Zoe had spoken her piece. "Letty tried, but she never could get close enough to find out."

"Letty?"

"Letty McFee." Billy Joe pulled a jacket from the peg by the door. "She passes along messages when she can." He began to stuff a variety of items into his jacket pockets. "The post office leaks information like a pail shot full of holes, but she gets some news from Hodge, too."

"She never!" said Zoe, remembering Letty's talk when they went berrying. "Because Mister Hodge is an Indian!"

Billy Joe smiled at Zoe, mistaking her confusion. "He's not the only Indian fighting for the cause. But Hodge figured he could do more good out of a uniform than in one."

"Mister Hodge is miles and miles away," protested Zoe. But she'd been wrong about Letty. Maybe she was mistaken about him, too. If Mister Hodge was hiding out in the woods all along, even tonight . . .

"He could not say for certain about any Yankee movement," Billy Joe continued, "so Letty promised to try to find out." Billy Joe pulled on the jacket. " 'Pears to have been your little brother who got the news soonest."

Zoe leaned against the doorjamb and shook her head. "Jim Henry surprises a lot of folks," she said.

"I'll be leaving for Kennesaw Mountain directly. I pledge you I'll get the word to General Johnston himself."

"You and Letty . . ." Zoe hesitated and then blurted, "Is that another pledge you're keeping?"

Billy Joe gaped at her. "How so?"

"Aren't you two—promised to marry?" asked Zoe.

Billy Joe threw back his head and laughed. Zoe was fearful he'd wake the baby in the cradle.

"You think that's why Letty came to call?" Billy Joe asked when he'd caught his breath. "Reckon it don't matter if you know. She was slipping me some quinine to take to the hospital wagons."

"Quinine!"

"We've precious little of it, and it's best for bringing down the fever."

"When we started off to berry, Letty wasn't carrying anything," objected Zoe, shifting her own bundle to her other arm.

"Not so's you'd notice," Billy Joe agreed. "But those fat curls of hers were wrapped around papers of quinine salts. She laid hold of them at the post office."

"Her Mama . . ." Zoe shook her head. "Didn't she suspect?"

"Missus McFee?" Billy Joe chuckled again. "She suspects everything, but she'll never prove anything."

Zoe looked at Billy Joe in the light from the sputtering candle. The shadowy stubble on his chin didn't appear to be bristly like pinfeathers. It was more like fluff on a chick. Zoe took his hand and shook it.

"Good luck, Billy Joe," she said and left.

The whitewashed picket fence that enclosed the Judsons' yard was bright in the moonlight. The fence was for show, not privacy, for it opened onto the pike to Hiawassee. By day that road was ugly mud, but now it unwound through the countryside like a pale silk sash. Zoe opened the gate and started north.

She couldn't get over Letty McFee. No wonder her bonnet had been askew when she returned from her delivery to Billy Joe. She was the last person in the world that Zoe would have picked as a courier, all decked out in her ruffles and kid shoes. "These days there's no knowing about anyone." That's what Mama had said.

Zoe balanced on the ridge of a rut, walking as if she were on a tightrope. She ticked off thoughts in time to her careful steps.

Left foot, Letty McFee. She'd never be another Emma Sanson, but Letty was a sort of heroine, too. Hadn't she sneaked into a yard full of Yankees, right in broad daylight?

Right foot, Zoe herself. She'd been the one to get the message about the Yanks attacking Kennesaw to Billy Joe. Still, that was only because Jim Henry happened to overhead and tell her.

Left foot. Zoe hadn't reasoned it out in advance. All she'd settled on was taking off like some ragtag deserter, and only she knew why.

Right foot, left foot, step, step, step. It was like the ticktock of the grandfather clock. That notion made her see Captain Hetcher's face, plain as the moon overhead. Too bad she'd not see his comeuppance when he dis-

132

covered she was gone! She tried to imagine that, but unexpectedly she saw Mama's face instead, white and pinched with worry.

Zoe teetered on the toe of one boot. A verse from *Proverbs* jingled in her head.

Any journey once begun
Must be continued till it's done.

"Flapdoodle!"

The voice was hers, unnaturally loud in the stillness of the night, but the word was Mama's. It just happened to come out. Of all the astonishing things she'd heard this day, that nonsense word was the one which mattered most.

Zoe turned and headed home. Mama needed her.

The returning seemed much slower than the going. Although she did not dawdle, the path zigzagged on and on, a maze through the woods. Brambles caught at her skirt, and small animals, unseen, skittered from underfoot. Now doubts, like buried tree roots, humped up in her mind.

First thing tomorrow she'd have to apologize to Captain Hetcher. Zoe Snyder, not the captain, would be the one to eat humble pie. Perhaps she'd have to crawl on her hands and knees and beg him not to burn the clock. He'd sneer at her. How she'd hate that! But she knew she'd like herself a whole lot better when she'd found the pluck to face him.

It was a coon's age before she reached the bridge and saw the outline of the well house. Joshua Boone did not stand in its shelter. He must have moved farther down creek, and Zoe was relieved. If he saw her come back alone, he'd know she'd not told the real reason for her errand. She'd not like him to think her untruthful, even if he was the enemy.

Zoe was too stirred up to go straight to bed. She huddled on the cabin doorstep, arms about her knees. Already the moon was getting low and the campfires had burned down to orange puddles of light. Zoe listened to the creek and yawned. The sound of the water, rinsing the pebbles, over and over again, made her sleepy.

A shriek tore the air. The cry was loud and sudden as an engine's whistle, but shriller, sadder. Everything alive in the night seemed to hold its breath, stunned by that scream into silence.

"A panther," Zoe whispered, "yowling at the moon." She shivered and said loudly, "No panther would dare come close, not with bonfires still burning."

One by one the normal night noises returned. A great horned owl sailed low and landed heavily in the sycamore by the well house. The wind ruffled the owl's feathers, but the bird sat motionless on its perch.

Owls were bad omens. Zoe looked down at the tortoise-shell talisman. It caught the moonlight and winked up at her like an eye. Joshua Boone had said how something went was up to you. Signs and charms could not change matters. He'd claim that fretting over bad-luck birds was childish and that the old owl was just tending to its business. Mousing.

She had her own business to tend to. Morning would come soon enough. Zoe picked up her sack, went into the cabin, and pulled the drawstring tight.

Thursday
19

"Wake up!"

Reluctantly, Zoe half opened her eyes, slitting her lids against the glare and squinting up at Jim Henry. It seemed she had scarcely been to sleep at all.

"Morning," she mumbled, and then opened her eyes wide. Sunshine! That's what was different about this morning. Sun shone through the cabin doorway, so brightly she could see dust motes dance above her head.

Something else was different about today as well, something that caught her ears, not her eyes. Zoe could hear men shouting, although she could not make out their words. Horses snorted and harness chains jangled, and there was a clatter as if all the pots and pans in creation were banging together. How could she have slept through such a racket?

136

Zoe leaned on one elbow. "What in heaven's name is going on?"

"Get all the way up," Jim Henry insisted.

The buttons on his jacket didn't match the holes. He must have dressed without help today. "Where's Mama?"

"Up at the house. They're leaving!"

Zoe sat bolt upright. "Who?"

"The Damnyankees. They're breaking camp. Captain's orders. 'Company, march!' " Jim Henry strutted around the room.

Zoe was fully awake now. "Why? For pity's sake, stay put a moment."

"Maybe it was our pulleybone. Maybe we wished up the whole thing."

"That was just tomfoolery—" Zoe began.

"No, sir, it wasn't. You can ask the captain hisself. He's been ranting on about it for hours and hours."

"About what? How come you were there to hear?"

"Morton promised to take me fishing. He said we had to wake when the fish did or we wouldn't hook nothing. Soon as the sky got light, I sneaked up to the house."

"You tell me all you heard, Jim Henry, each and every word."

"Well"—Jim Henry sat on the chair and swung his feet—"it 'pears Captain Itch went to bed last night, same as always. But maybe he forgot to tell his prayers, because pretty soon he hears this fearful scream."

Zoe hugged her knees. "A panther. I heard it caterwauling, too."

"Maybe that's what it was," her brother allowed, but he looked annoyed by her interruption. "Anyhow, *something* woke the captain. So he jumps out of bed and runs to the window and what do you suppose he saw?"

"The counterpane?"

"An Indian! Captain claims he glowed, all shiny with bear grease, and he had great big white circles drawn 'round his eyes." Jim Henry made circles with his fingers and peered through them at Zoe.

"Go on," she urged.

"It was the eyes made Captain Hetcher know that the Indian *wasn't* . . . *even* . . . *human!*" Jim Henry drew out the words.

Zoe caught her breath. "Why?"

"Its eyes were dead. That's what the captain said. Pale-yellow eyeballs. He says everybody knows that Injuns got black eyes. This one had to be a haunt!"

"What did the captain do then?"

"It's what the spook did! When he sees the captain staring out the window at him, he opens his mouth and . . ." Jim Henry threw back his head and howled, ". . . Ca-wa-no-dee!"

Zoe's own mouth dropped open in disbelief. That was a Cherokee war cry! Or as near to it as Jim Henry could come. Right off she thought of Mister Hodge, but the picture didn't fit. Last she'd seen he was wearing a top hat and frock coat. "What happened?" she asked.

"Old Itch grabs his boots and throws one right through the window at the spook."

"Did it break?"

"How could a boot sail clean through glass without breaking it?"

Mama's beautiful window with the stained-glass border! Zoe shut her mouth so fast she nicked her tongue.

"Then he busts out the door, but that ghost had just plumb disappeared." Jim Henry waved an arm. "Whoosh!"

"But—" Zoe began.

Her brother ignored her. "Then, when the captain tries to get back into the house, the kitchen door had latched itself shut. And the front door was bolted. So there he was in the yard, in his nightshirt! And yelling like the bejabbers."

"You never did hear Captain Hetcher admit any such thing."

"Well, not the last part. Morton told me that. He's the one who had to come down and let the captain in. Boone was gone someplace."

"He was standing sentry," Zoe blurted and then added quickly, "It sounds like the captain got moonstruck."

"Maybe he got some corn juice instead. That's what Morton figures."

Zoe lay down again. "And now Captain Hetcher's leaving? I can hardly believe it."

"Course you do. You're the one who said the captain's scared of ghosts." Jim Henry tugged at the bedclothes. "Come on, Zoe. You fixing to lie there all day?"

Zoe ran up the lane after her brother. They passed half a dozen men cussing at wagons stuck in the mud

139

and tugging at the reins of balky mules. Jim Henry waved at them. Then he stopped suddenly. "Zoe!" he wailed. "I never said good-bye to Sergeant Morton!"

Zoe kept on running. She had seen Captain Hetcher as soon as she'd reached the rise in the lane. He was astride his Morgan horse by the veranda steps. The captain wore both sword and sidearm, but his feet were shod in ordinary ankle-high boots. Zoe looked about. Apparently Captain Hetcher was the last of the Yankees to leave. Neither Morton nor Joshua Boone was anywhere in sight. Only Mama stood on the veranda. Zoe hesitated at the edge of the drive.

"Captain Hetcher and his unit are departing," Mama called, unable to hide her pleasure.

"The weather's cleared," the captain explained, "so I gave marching orders a little sooner than I'd planned." He touched a gloved hand to his hat. "I shall never forget, ma'am, the most . . . peculiar . . . hospitality that your home offered."

Mama nodded politely, puzzled, and Captain Hetcher turned to Zoe. "I daresay you've no objections to our going."

Zoe looked at him directly. "No, sir," she said.

Their eyes held and locked for a moment. Then the captain dropped his gaze and spat on the muddy drive. "Little witch!" He kicked the Morgan sharply in the flanks, and horse and rider took off down the lane like they were chased by demons.

Zoe watched until they'd disappeared around the bend and then she joined her mother on the veranda.

Mama rested her head on Zoe's shoulder. "I could never have stood it without you," she said.

Zoe could feel wetness soak through her sleeve. Mama was crying. Then her mother straightened and wiped her hands on her apron, as if removing the last stain and smell of Yankee from her fingers.

"Zoe," Mama said briskly, "I want the house aired out straightaway. We'll boil the sheets and burn a sulphur candle in the bedrooms. I know Bluecoats have got bedbugs!"

Zoe grinned at Jim Henry. Mama was back to her usual self.

Thursday
20

In her mind's eye, Zoe had seen the clock afire so often that she was almost surprised to find it standing, straight-backed as always, guarding the hall. But the pendulum was still. Given a push, it would swing back and forth but once or twice and then stop.

Mama shook her head. "I don't know what's got into that timepiece."

"Me," whispered Jim Henry to Zoe, but Mama didn't hear.

"It could use an oiling, after all that smoke. Your father can see to it when—whenever."

Zoe smiled at Mama. It was better to have a secret with her than from her. She followed her mother down the hall as they continued their grim inspection.

The window set with rainbow glass was shattered

beyond repair, and they had to stuff the frame with rags. A good thing that the weather was promising.

In Mama's parlor, they found a burn in the sofa cushion, and the horsehair stuffing poked out the hole. A crack ran the length of the blue vase, and one of the silver spoons, left on the table, had been bent round like a bracelet.

It looked like a tornado had blown right through Papa's parlor. The chair was upended, and the books had been jerked from the shelves and scattered about the floor. It was plain that Captain Hetcher had planned to search and perhaps burn them all had he not departed so hastily. But the most important papers and Mama's wedding ring were safe in their niche behind the bricks. The ivory-handled letter opener stuck straight up from the desktop, its tip embedded in the wood. When Zoe pulled it out, it left an ugly, raw gouge.

"Now why on earth would he do that?" wondered Mama, rubbing at the deep dent with her finger.

Mama worked as if possessed. Zoe's arms ached from toting buckets of soapy water. Together, they scoured the entire downstairs, and now the smell was of lye, not cigar smoke. Only once did her mother criticize her, and that was when Zoe was sweeping the parlor, erasing the telltale gray ashes from the blue carpet.

"Always sweep toward the fireplace, never toward the door," she cautioned.

"Why, Mama!" Zoe replied. "Don't be superstitious!"

Mama's jaw dropped. "Seems to me you're the one

who . . ." She shrugged. "Never mind. Help me do up my bed."

Mama's bed was beaten until the feathers fairly burst through the ticking. The linens were changed, and the counterpane, dry at last, was tucked on top. Zoe found one of Captain Hetcher's shiny high-top boots beneath the dust ruffle. Jim Henry found the mate when they went out into the yard to pick up the broken glass. It was half hidden beneath the yellow bellbush, thrown so hard it had dug itself heel first into the mud.

Jim Henry immediately laid claim to the boots. When he'd pulled them on, they reached almost waist high. "Attention!" he ordered, parading stiffly around the yard, unable to bend his knees.

Zoe almost told him to take them off and save them for Papa, but she thought better of it. They'd likely be too small for her father, and Jim Henry had surely earned them.

Her brother stopped marching so suddenly he almost toppled over. "Zo!" he exclaimed. "Can haunts leave footprints?"

Zoe didn't reply. She busied herself picking up shards of colored glass and dropping them with a clatter into the bucket. How had he found out? And how could she make her attempts to leave ghostly tracks sound anything but silly?

"Looky over here, Zo." Jim Henry wasn't looking at her. He pointed with the toe of his boot beneath the hawthorn tree. Close to the trunk were two deep, distinct moccasin prints. "Did a ghost do that?"

144

Zoe stared, feeling prickles rise along the back of her neck. "I'm not sure," she said. "That's a question only Captain Hetcher can answer."

Zoe got Jim Henry to help her carry their belongings back from Hodge's cabin. On their final trip up to the house, they left the lane to look at the cornfield where the soldiers had camped. The Yankees had left broken utensils, spent shells, and a vast variety of rubbish behind. Jim Henry's pockets soon sagged with treasures.

Her brother nudged the fallen scarecrow with his boot. "I wish they hadn't gone off before Mister Mort took me fishing," he said.

If that didn't beat all! Mister Mort and the mosquito! "Someone else will take you fishing soon," Zoe promised.

"Who? You? You're too skeered of worms to bait the hook."

Creepy-crawlies still made her stomach knot up, but she need not admit it to Jim Henry. "I had a different person in mind," she replied, and changed the subject. "Look. We might plant some snap beans here. Ashes help break up the clay."

Jim Henry wrinkled his nose. "And manure! Haw! Those Yankees left us piles and piles of manure."

"That's quite enough of that, young man," Zoe said, picking up the basket of clothes again. Good heavens! she thought. I'm beginning to sound just like Mama. And to prove she wasn't all that grown-up, she added, "Race you up to the house!"

She caught the kitchen door so that it would not bang behind them. Mama's own door was closed so she must be lying down.

"Ssssh!" Zoe put a warning finger to her lips. "Mama's wore out."

Jim Henry nodded. He stomped out into the yard to poke about for other abandoned prizes. Zoe took the clothes basket upstairs. She dumped Jim Henry's belongings on his bed and checked the spare room. The sergeant must have been in a terrible hurry, because the room was in an unholy mess, but hungry Morton had never discovered the ham!

Her own room was as tidy as if no one had stayed in it at all. The water had been emptied from the washbasin and no telltale yellow whiskers clung to the rim. She might have made up Joshua Boone, for all the evidence he'd left. Except for the tortoise-shell talisman, hanging about her neck. He had left that. Zoe polished the shell with her shirt sleeve. That Yankee had left her something else besides: a whole lot of things to ponder.

She put her clothes in the chest and dropped her journal on top. One of the pages from *Proverbs* slipped out, and she picked it up. It was the page with the verse she'd copied. But she'd written it down wrong. She'd gotten it backwards, for it ended,

> *If there be one, try to find it.*
> *If there be none, never mind it.*

Things might have been different if she'd gotten it right. Then the final words going round in her head would have been *never mind it*. She wouldn't have even tried to make ghostly tracks, wouldn't have ruined Mama's slippers. But she *wasn't* responsible for those moccasin prints by the hawthorn tree!

Well, she'd never mind it *now*. Zoe crumpled up the page from *Proverbs* and picked up the brass-tipped pen. She inked it carefully and wrote in bold black letters:

Thursday, June 23, 1864
Today the enemy has gone.

Friday
21

Zoe was supposed to fill the pitchers on the washstands and empty the chamber pots beneath the beds. She was going to do it, too, much as she despised the chore. But pitchers and pots wouldn't walk away. They could just wait until she'd written in her journal. An idea had come to her in the night.

Friday, June 24, 1864
I still hope for a baby sister, name of Emma. But should she be a boy, I've a name picked out for him as well.

JOHN HODGE SNYDER
That should make both Papa and the baby proud, and it would be a proper welcome, whichever one of them gets here first. I think that Mama, once she has had time to consider, will find it fitting, too.

Jim Henry should take to that name, for the two brothers would share the same initials: J.H.S. When they are bigger, then they can swap handkerchiefs, for one monogram will do for both.

I take pleasure in the name for special reasons of my own.

That was all she intended to put down, for the moment at least. Her journal had turned out to be as curious as that old *Proverbs* book, and she'd best take care what she said. Papa had been right. The written word was all-fired important. Zoe knew that firsthand. She'd had another notion late last night, and the thought was so surprising it kept her eyes wide open till daylight.

Mister Hodge had been the mysterious visitor! It was his own cabin, after all. He'd read her words, so just by putting down that she was trying to fix things for Captain Hetcher, she'd fixed up something else to happen. Hodge figured she needed his help, and who else could have spooked the captain like that? Unless . . . unless somehow she'd called up a genuine ghost to send Captain Hetcher off, coattails flying!

Zoe put the thought from her mind. Whatever, she was not about to write anything, ever again, that might come back to haunt her. Besides, and she was dead certain of this, Jim Henry would sneak a look in her journal any chance he got.

She could see her brother in the yard right now, taking the whole place apart, leaf by stalk, looking for the nest that biddy had hid. He was saying something, singing, but she couldn't rightly tell what. Zoe opened the window.

"The old gray mare, she ain't what she used to be,
Ain't what she used to be,
Ain't what she used to be . . ."

Where in heaven had he learned that? Morton, she could bet.

". . . Many long years ago-o-o!"

What was that buzzing over her head? A bee!

It must have flown up from the honeysuckle. She'd forgotten the honeysuckle bush, forgotten about Mama's slippers hidden beneath it. Peculiar that Jim Henry had not discovered them, with all his poking about. Zoe ducked, swatting the air with her book.

"Hallelujah!" It was only a fly. A fat old bluebottle. "Shoo, fly, don't bother me. . . ."

When had Jim Henry sung *that* song? Just last Saturday. But this had to be the longest week that ever was. Many long days ago. A whole month of seven days.

The fly landed on her nose. If a fly lands on your nose, somebody has something to tell you. But she was the one with the telling to do. Sooner or later she'd have to explain to Mama about the ruined shoes, and about everything else.

Zoe clapped her hands. "Ab-ra-ca-da-bra!" she chanted.

The fly bobbled dizzily overhead and then flew straight out the window.

Zoe dropped the journal and took stock of herself in the mirror. She did not look like a witch, 'cepting for those strands of hair that had escaped the curling rags and were sticking out, stiff as porcupine quills. She was going to need a whole lot more practice before she could twist her hair into fat curls like Letitia Jane McFee's.

"Zoe!" Mama called up the stairwell.

Zoe sighed and picked up the water pitcher. How did her mother always know when she wasn't doing what she should be? "Yes'm?" she said.

"Zoe," Mama repeated, not sounding all that cross. "Would you go cross creek and fetch Sallie Judson? I think I'll be needing her soon."

An Afterword to
Zoe Snyder's Journal

Wednesday, June 29, 1864

Two days ago, early in the morning, the Battle of Kennesaw Mountain began. Our Confederate forces, led by General Joe Johnston, were expecting the Yankee attack, and had fortifications in place on the plain of the hill. According to Mrs. Postmaster McFee, the Union forces, under General William Tecumseh Sherman, were decisively thrown back.

Now we wait for Papa, the four of us: Mama, Jim Henry, myself, and our new brother. Mama let me choose the name. John Hodge Snyder is fitting, she says. When Papa comes, I think he will agree.

Zoe Snyder, her family, and her neighbors are all imaginary, but Emma Sanson was a real heroine. Letty's device of smuggling medicine in her curls is based upon an actual incident, and Mister Hodge's action is characteristic of Indian participation in the war. Thousands of Indians served in both Union and Confederate forces. Throughout this book, the songs, the weather, even the phase of the moon, are just as Zoe Snyder might have recorded them in her journal.

The Battle of Kennesaw Mountain was the last that the South won in the War Between the States, and Sherman claimed his ill-timed attack was the only military mistake he ever made. The battlefield is now a national monument.